HAPPINESS AND HEARTBREAK

An Anthology of Irish-Themed

Short Stories, Plays, and Poetry by

Known and Unkown Writers

WIL ARNOLD • THOMAS LUKE HAUGHTON • WILLIAM LEECE • TOMMY MURRAY • CATHERINE RATCLIFFE • KRISTIN RICHARDS • HELEN ROWNTREE • LARRY WILSON • TOM RICHARDS

Authors Innovation
1 Ivy Lane Wallington NJ
Wallington NJ. 070577

Contents

DEDICATION

This anthology is dedicated to

Bill Leece

Friend, educator, and scholar, he is a lover of Irish culture and all things Irish. Bill has recently retired from Rolling Meadows High School, District 214, near Chicago, Illinois, USA. Bill's short story is proudly published
as part of this anthology.

A special Note from Tom Richards to all readers: this Anthology is composed of a variety of short-stories, poetry and plays most having an Irish Theme. Toward the end of this volume is a white paper on Writing a Bestselling Novel for Online Publication. This paper tells all would-be authors of how to write a novel for the screen, stage, and online publication. Will your work be produced or result in a bestselling novel? To answer the question, do what I do: put your bum in the seat, turn on your computer or tap on your typewriter and get started! That's all you have to do to see if you have what it takes! All my best wishes,

Tom Richards Eyeries, Beara, Bantry, County Cork, Ireland
www.tomrichards.ie
tomrichards141@gmail.com May, 2022

Happiness & Heartbreak

A Short Story by Tom Richards

This unplanned trip begins with happy expectations and ends in wild bewilderment.

My name is Christopher Nelson. I'm an American, a mere sixty-seven, who has lived in Ireland for the past twenty-odd years. For the last eleven or so, I've lived in Eyeries Village on the Beara Peninsula, a stunning location in Ireland's rugged southwest. Having retired, I moved down to this remote spot to write fiction and, prior to taking the holiday, published my first Irish romantic fantasy novel for women, a book that quickly went to global Number 1 and attracted the attention of a number of film producers. A recovering alcoholic, I didn't need that attention. I was plagued by phone calls, and late-night knocks at the front door. When I opened it, reporters thrust their tape recorders in my face, and cameras flashed as they sought to interview this unknown writer who wanted to be left alone. Deciding to escape, I climbed into a borrowed car, a brand-new black Ford Ranger pickup truck I'd borrowed from Ger, my best friend, and sped out of the village unnoticed by the gang of unruly paparazzi still gathered in front of my home.

I've always loved lighthouses. I've used them as a theme for many books, and because their light always lit my soul, their glittering magical beams always made me refuse the next drink. After all, what they say is true: it's the first drink that leads to many more and has nothing to do with the volume a person drinks. So many get that wrong, which is why I'm so careful and, after a failed marriage, now live alone.

With the crowd of reporters left behind, I headed due north, along the coastline and through the tourist town of Kenmare. There, I turned west and kept going. My final destination was a small fishing village located on Valentia Island just off the Ring of Kerry, a beautiful area I'd always wanted to visit.

Portmagee is a wonderful village. Nestled against an active fishing harbor, the town boasts many things, including a national award for the Best Public Toilet in Ireland, which I still find a hoot. Seriously, though, the place is a delight. On the eastern end, a two-lane expansion bridge thrusts out over the open water leading to Valentia Island and the lighthouse I wanted to visit. The village has a single main street dotted with shops that look like something out of a Dickens novel: window displays are filled with knickknacks, including model lighthouses, caps, mugs, and keyrings, most of them stamped with a Valentia Lighthouse Logo. The post office also acts as a village shop. In the summer, long blue and white boats filled with tourists steam out to Skellig Michael, a prime location for a recent *Star Wars* film. When the moon shines on the harbor, just like the lighthouse, it lights my soul. I'd seen Portmagee on the map and, noting its stunning location, wanted to spend the night there prior to my lighthouse visit. But as I drove further west, first through the Ring of Kerry towns of Sneem and Waterville, it dawned on me that I had neglected to book a room at Portmagee's only bar, restaurant, and B&B, The Moorings. With the sun going down early because it was just before Christmas, I decided to phone, but as I searched through the pickup, it dawned on me that I'd been in such a rush to escape from the throng of reporters that I'd left my cell phone on a table next to the front door. The only thing I could do was keep going. So I grabbed a cup of coffee at a shop just past Waterville and kept driving north. Then thick fog descended along the Kerry Coastline, and I got lost. I drove for miles out of my way before stopping to ask a local for directions. An old farmer wearing a thick yellow work coat who was walking home pointed me on, and I knew I was on the right track, but again, I got lost.

Now, it was past six thirty in the evening and completely black. During winter in Ireland, the sun goes down at about four thirty. I turned off the radio and decided I had no other option but to turn around and go back home to Eyeries. But then I saw to my left a bright light and realized it was the Valentia Lighthouse. According to a paper map I'd bought along with my cup of coffee, it was located only five miles or so from Portmagee. So I put my foot down and turned left toward the coast. Rounding a bend, I finally saw a string of pearls: beautiful white lights that lined the bridge heading across the strait from Portmagee to Valentia Island. My spine tingled at the sight.

When I arrived in the village, I found I'd been lucky. Because it was Christmas, most of the rooms in The Mooring were booked. But the owner, Vicky, took pity on me and gave me the very last room. I felt like I was Joseph, escorting the Virgin Mary riding on her donkey, because I'd learned that there was room at the inn for me.

Entering Room One, I discovered that my lodgings were perfect: a big soft bed with warm blankets and four fluffy pillows—it was much too large for me. A color television would keep me occupied when I wasn't reading or working on the notes for my latest novel (I had a pending deadline), and there was a big bathroom with a full shower—even a hair dryer, though I had no hair. I thought as I turned it on, feeling its warmth, that all I needed was a woman, but I kicked myself, assuring myself that I was fine without a female partner. After all, I had been single for years.

I opened my bag, putting away my belongings. Shirt and trousers went into a long, narrow closet. Socks, underwear, and T-shirts were stuffed into a bureau. I laid my laptop on top of a conveniently large rolltop desk and, sitting down, was intent on getting to work.

But then the room phone rang. It was Vicky inviting me down to dinner. It was almost 11:00 p.m., and if I was coming I had to make reservations for the last sitting. Deciding to go because I was finally hungry, I gathered my coat, put on my hat, and—taking my room key—walked the two flights of steps downstairs.

In the dining room, I ordered something that tasted like spaghetti, an Italian dish created by Vicky's husband, Chef Willy. Man, was it good. I'd decided not to have the turkey and bacon, which I decided to save for the next night. After all, I thought, tomorrow is Christmas Eve. Why not save the best for that hallowed night? Little did I know as I finished my dinner that another surprise awaited me, and in fact I was saving the best for last.

Then I looked up and saw *her*. Tegan Brady O'Shea looked like an angel. Her short, curling brown hair was a halo lit from behind by a Christmas tree. Fathomless blue eyes gazed down on the guests seated at the next table as she took their order. Tegan's smile dimpled her smooth face, and her breasts looked so fresh, as if they'd never been touched.

When I looked at her, my resolve to remain single vanished. I had fallen in love at first sight, a depth of love I'd never known before, and something I thought teenagers only did. I could feel my cheeks burning, my heart swelling in my breast, and all I could feel was its loud thumping. When I decided to go out of my way to say hello, something I rarely said to a woman so much younger than me, I realized: she looked to be only forty-six. If I introduced myself, she'd think I was being fresh. After all, why would a guy aged sixty-seven be after anything other than sex? But if she thought that, she had to know she was wrong. I'd fallen off my emotional wagon. I was in love, hook, line, and sinker and I thought myself a fool.

Done taking the older couple's order, she drifted toward me like a heavenly creature. When she gazed down on me, I guessed how tall she was. I'm five-foot-six. She had to be almost six inches taller. Then I realized: it was her long legs that made her look taller. It turned out, when I asked her later, that she was only five-foot-eight.

When Tegan finished taking my order, I did what I had not done in over thirty years.

"Tegan," I called, "can I have a pint?" When she nodded and smiled, I realized it was not only my heart that had fallen off the wagon. I knew then and there that I was truly fucked.

When I had finished that single pint and went back to my room, my heart was racing. I vowed then and there never to drink again, not if I was going to attract Tegan or be able to live with myself. As I turned on my laptop to work on my novel, a plan boiled into my head. I started searching the Internet for an appropriate gesture to express my true feelings. 'But what are those feelings, exactly?' I thought as I glanced through various websites. When my Internet search ended, I found myself gazing at the image of a ring. But not just any old ring. It was a gold, emerald, and diamond engagement ring.

***

The next morning, I skipped breakfast, intent on my quest to buy that ring. I walked across the car park and climbed back into the pickup, which I'd fondly named the Beast, it was so big. Starting the truck, I glanced at my watch, an expensive Tissot, which John, my son from my failed marriage, had bought me for Christmas three years ago with money he had earned as a part-time salesman in an auto parts store in America. He had stopped talking to me shortly after that when I'd gotten drunk during the only Adult Softball game I'd ever attended. Having flown to Boston from Ireland to visit him where he lived with his Mom, I had attended a game to cheer on my then nineteen-year-old son. He was playing first base, and when he came to bat in the second inning and whacked the ball with all his might, I thought it was a home run. But when the umpire called my son's hit a foul, I stomped from the stands and confronted the official. I'd already drunk two six-packs of Bud that I'd snuck into the stands as well as a fifth of Scotch. As I screamed my objections, the burley ump's cheeks had turned bright red. And when I struck him in his ugly face, I shouldn't have been surprised when he called the cops. As I was led away, handcuffed, I looked back to see my son slouching toward the dugout, shoulders drooped with embarrassment. It was the last time I ever saw him, but someday I hope to make amends to both John and his mother, Liz. All I had to do was stay off the drink and keep working.

Still sitting in the truck, and with the horrific memory waning, I glanced down at the pilot's chronographer on my wrist. Its blue strap exactly matched the color of an old airplane I used to own in the States. When I thought of the airplane, another terrible memory came flooding into my head. After the above drunken incident with my son at the softball field, the next day, after I'd managed to call my U.S. lawyer to have him bail me out, I drove my rental car to Norwood Regional Airport, just south of Boston. Hungover and with a head that felt like it was on fire, I'd managed to somehow rent a Cessna 150, a single engine trainer, with an old pilot's license that had expired long ago. That morning, I had used a black pen to update the paper license, making it current. The guy who had rented me the Cessna didn't glance twice at it. Instead, he asked me how many hours I had flown in the last month and I told him ten hours in a Cessna 172, a plane somewhat bigger than the 150, which was a complete lie. He took a deposit then handed me the keys, and helped me with the walk-around of the trainer. Satisfied that I seemed to know what I was doing, he left me to it as I climbed into the small cockpit and started her up.

Having received clearance from the airfield's control tower, I was clear-headed enough to taxi the aircraft to the end of the active runway. But I forgot to get clearance to taxi onto it. As I advanced the throttle and gained airspeed for take-off, I heard the control tower in my headphones ordering me to stop. But it was too late because I had just lifted off the ground. That's when I happened to glance up. A twin-engine Beechcraft King Air, which had been on final approach, flew right over me. We were so close I could see the angry look on the pilot's face as he sat in the cockpit. Startled, I pulled up to miss the King Air, but much too sharply. The Cessna 150 staggered over Interstate 95 then stalled and spun, and crashed in Reservoir Pond, a few miles from the airport. As I extracted myself from the plane, I stood on a broken wing, waiting to be rescued by local fishermen. When I was picked up, I watched as the blue-and-white Cessna sank to the bottom. It was my closest encounter with death, one I'll never, ever forget. That, and the bill for the expensive Cessna. Too, I was examined a few months later by the National Transportation and Safety Board which discovered that my pilot's license had expired. I knew then that I would never fly as a pilot again.

Still sitting in my pickup, I glanced down at the Tissot watch, which reminded me of that incident every time I looked at it, as well as my son's indifference to his alcoholic dad. It read 7:10 a.m., which explained why the fishing town was so quiet. Not a soul stirred in the streets. Only the squawk of seagulls fishing for breakfast accompanied me and my memories as I started the Beast and sped out of Portmagee. As I glanced again at my map, I realized I didn't need it anymore. The single coastal road would lead me first to Waterville, then on to Sneem, that day's final destination.

***

When I arrived again in Waterville, I parked my car at a local public car park that overlooked the Atlantic. I stood for a good fifteen minutes to take in the stunning view of rollers crashing onto the rocky beach. The sky was filled with low cumulous cloud, and the sun was well over the yardarm—it was only 8:30 a.m. by my precious watch—a time I'd always started drinking beer when I was married and an active alcoholic. By noon I'd have consumed at least 3 six-packs of beer and a bottle of vodka. But I shook off the memories of my past addiction again and strolled over to the public toilets quite close by. After relieving myself, I watched the dogs at play on the beach, led along by their masters. It made me think of Kelly, my son's border collie, and how I'd accidentally killed it when backing the car out of our home's driveway, smashed again on a gram or two of coke and a bottle of wine.

Forget about it, I scolded myself. Didn't you promise that someday soon you'd make amends to your ex-wife and son? Scanning the peninsula north of Waterville, in the direction of Portmagee, I couldn't help but again think of Tegan and the decision I had made. Climbing back into my Beast, I headed east. Next stop: Sneem and some Christmas shopping.

It took only forty-five minutes to drive to the town, a gateway of sorts to the Ring of Kerry. I stopped for a minute at a lay-by and gazed south. From my vantage point overlooking a now-quiet sea, I made out the island of Skellig Michael, the largest of the Skellig Islands. From where I stood, the real Atlantic began, and there, the waves smashed onto the rocky fortress of Michael, billowing high in white ghosts of sea spray. Following that, I climbed back into the Beast and continued toward Sneem.

Having arrived in the town, I took a long walk. Because it was Christmas Eve, I decided to start by purchasing a handful of presents for Tegan. In the first shop, a small jewelry store, I asked the sales attendant to show me the selection of engagement rings, but I didn't think Tegan would fancy any of them. Instead, I selected a fine watch, a gold Seiko, which she could wear when she waitressed. I waited as the shop attendant wrapped the black watch box in wonderful Christmas paper and then strode out the door to see what else the town had to offer.

The next stop was a tourist shop. There, I bought Tegan a pair of earrings, a warm hat and scarf, and a comfortable pair of slippers shaped like a black dog, which I thought she'd find cute. I still hadn't found the engagement ring, and suspected I'd have to drive all the way back to Kenmare to buy it. Clutching my packages, I headed back to the pickup. As I again walked past the jewelry shop, something sparked in the morning sunlight. Stepping to the window, I saw a wonderful ring hidden among watches and necklace boxes. Opening the front door, I strode once again inside.

"You're back again?" the lovely shopkeep asked. "Did you forget something?"

"No, it's not that. I was hoping to see a ring you have in the window."

She walked to the window display and pointed at the various pieces of jewelry. "That one?" she asked.

"No, the next one down."

Her hand settled on the ring box, and as she withdrew it and turned toward me, I could see that it was the ring of my dreams. She pulled it out of its box and as she did, explained it to me. "This is the Ring of Kerry," she said. "It was created by our jeweler, the owner of the shop, from a single block of silver." She turned it in her hand and pointed out the glittering gems. "These are twin sapphires," she explained. "They're special because they were mined right here in Kerry."

Taking it from her, I realized that the jewels perfectly matched the sparkling blue eyes of my newly-found love.

"This is perfect," I whispered, slipping it on my left ring finger. "I'll take it."

"Is she with you?" the shopkeep asked. "It would be much better if she could try it on herself."

I grinned and decided to tell a white lie. "Tegan's the only woman I've ever met who I can buy for right off the peg. Jeans that I purchase online even fit." Again, I glanced down at the sparkling jewels. "Her ring finger is exactly the same size as mine."

As she wrapped it in Christmas paper, I realized that my Christmas shopping was done.

***

Back at the hotel, I readied myself for the shocking proposal I was determined to make that night after I ate dinner, one that Tegan would never suspect was coming. As if preparing for a military inspection, I made myself ready. First the shower with the second shave of the day. I also gave my bald head a close shave with my Mach III. After toweling myself dry, I doused myself in aftershave. That done, I strode back into the bedroom and straight to the wardrobe. I took out my best attire: a fresh pair of jeans, a black T-Shirt, and a flannel shirt I'd purchased a year ago online from Pendleton. Finally, I put on my best pair of boots. Inspecting myself in the room's full-length mirror, I hoped I didn't look like an actor out of a western TV series—say *Rawhide*. Having passed the close inspection, I went downstairs to eat, convinced that Tegan could only say yes to the ring that I held in my hand. Glancing back at the bed, I made sure the two bunches of yellow roses that I'd bought after buying the ring were well positioned in back of the Christmas presents. It made the entire room look like Santa had already visited despite the early hour of only 8:00 p.m.

That night the dining room was packed, but despite that, Tegan had saved me my old seat. I sat and ordered steak and a bottle of wine. I placed the ring box on the table just to gaze at it. Then another waitress by the name of Caroline strode over to take my order. I declined the offer of a pint of Guinness and instead ordered only water. She glanced at the box and asked what was inside. I scanned the room, making certain that Tegan was out of sight.

"It's an engagement ring," I stated, not able to hide my nervous smile.

"An engagement ring. For who?" Caroline asked.

At that moment, Tegan appeared, serving a family of four right next to me. I had to lower my voice. "For her," I stated, pointing at the girl of my dreams.

"For Tegan?" Caroline yelped.

I placed an index finger to my lips, wanting to keep the moment private. Rather than say a word, I nodded my head yes.

"Does she suspect anything?" Caroline continued.

"I hope so," I said. "She has to know how I feel. Every time I look at her, she smiles back with a special look that must be meant only for me."

Caroline leaned across the table toward me, her eyes filled with conspiracy. "When and where do you plan to do the deed?"

"I'm not sure. Any ideas?"

She glanced at her watch. "Tegan's due a break in ten minutes. How about during her break, in there?"

She pointed to the back of the room. Behind a closed door were the toilets. To the left was another door, and beyond that, the break room. I'd never been in there.

"It's always quiet in there," Caroline continued. "Guests aren't allowed in. Only staff."

"Tegan has her break ten minutes from right now?" I asked, gulping at my glass of water.

"Ten minutes," Caroline answered. Her smile expanded into a grin as her eyebrows thrust upward to heaven.

***

When I got back to my room after seeing Caroline and her plan of ambush in the break room, I began to get ready with military precision. First another long shower, and while I was in there, I shaved my face twice and also my bald head again. Getting out, I toweled myself dry, then applied a heavy dose of aftershave all over my body. Finished, I took a look in the mirror. I still looked sixty-seven, not twenty-six as I'd hoped when I started my toilet.

Padding back to the bedroom in my bare feet, I walked directly to the closet. I pulled out my best cotton shirt, a fresh pair of jeans, new underwear which I had bought yesterday in Sneem along with a black T-shirt, and my best brown wingtip shoes. Having dressed, I looked in the room's full-length mirror.

Okay, I thought to myself. I still don't look twenty-six, but it'll have to do.

Finished getting ready, I glanced at the wide double bed. The fresh roses still lay side-by-side, framing the Christmas gifts. Then I put her ring box in my shirt pocket and slipped from the room, locking the door firmly behind me.

When I arrived at the restaurant, it was still packed. It had taken me twenty minutes to get ready, not ten as Caroline had commanded. I fingered the slim package in my shirt and, stepping shakily toward the back door, opened it and peered through the window. Tegan sat at a table, her face shrouded in cigarette smoke. She drank a glass of fruit juice, and I was glad. If she'd had a glass of brandy, I would have ordered a bottle; I was that excited about my pending proposal. It dawned on me then that I was convinced Tegan would only say yes.

As I stepped toward the door that would take me into the staff break room, someone tapped me gently on the shoulder. I turned around. Yvonne, the hotel receptionist, stood stock still behind me, frowning. She pointed through the window.

"Caroline told me you're going to ask Tegan to marry you?" She tapped the slim lump in my shirt pocket. "Let me guess. That's the engagement ring Caroline also told me about."

I nodded, grinning. "You know it. Tegan is going to say yes. She's as excited as I am."

"How can you be so certain?" Yvonne asked. "Christ, didn't anyone tell you about Tegan?"

"Tell me. Tell me what?"

Yvonne leaned toward me. "It's a secret. I'm the only one in the hotel to know this. If I tell you, do you promise not to tell anyone else?"

"Of course I do. What are you talking about?"

"Tegan," she whispered, nodding toward my would-be fiancé. "She's gay not straight."

I rocked back on my heels at the news. "Gay? She can't be gay. Look at her."

My girl still sat at the table, looking anything but butch. Her hair sparkled like diamonds. Tegan's nails were painted a bright color to match the Christmas occasion. To me she looked the very definition of femininity. "Yvonne, you're wrong. Okay, Tegan isn't married, but many people choose not to marry. Look at me. I'm no longer married, and I'm not gay."

"Christ," she whispered again, taking my arm. "Hasn't anyone told you never to judge a book by its cover? Tegan has a female partner. Her name is Grace."

"Grace? But Grace is a woman's name."

"Grace is Tegan's wife."

"They're married?"

"Two years ago, in Paris. They went there so no one else would know. Except me. I stood as their witness. They didn't want anyone else there because they wanted a secret wedding. Because I was the only witness to their marriage vows, I'm the one who signed the license."

I swallowed thick bile that crept into the back of my throat and tried to hide my self-loathing for being an idiot. I felt sick and thought of running to the toilet to puke. "Why didn't Tegan tell me? Does she think I'm that untrustworthy?"

"For God's sake, you only met her yesterday, didn't you?" Yvonne laughed. "How could she think you are untrustworthy when she doesn't even know you?" She stepped away from me. "I'm sorry. You took a chance. A big one. It's just one of those things. Sometimes things work out; sometimes they don't."

"But so many people are gay, and they don't keep it hidden," I yelped. "Doesn't Tegan realize that by keeping her relationship a secret, she's being disrespectful to Grace? What does Grace do for a living, anyway?"

"She's the managing director and owner of an IT company."

"Grace is?" I yelped again. "And Tegan doesn't want even her friends at work to know? Tegan should be proud of her wife, not keep her hidden behind a cloud of secrecy."

Yvonne shrugged. "That's how Tegan wants to play it. I'm sorry. I hope you'll get over her."

I almost said something rude. "Oh, I'll get over her all right. A bitch like that? We talked. Why didn't she tell me?"

"Come on. Don't be like that."

"She broke my heart, don't you get it?" I took the ring box out of my pocket and thrust it at Yvonne. "Here, you take it. It'll look better on you than on the finger of a liar and a thief too."

"What do you mean, a thief?"

"If we'd married, I would have given her half of everything. That's called a binding marriage contract. Unlike what she would have given me. One lie after another."

When Yvonne refused to take the ring box, I slung it against the toilet door. I never wanted to see it again. I stormed back into the restaurant and once again considered buying a pint, I was so upset. But my resolve was set. I'd already fallen off the emotional wagon. I'd never fall off any other wagon again. All I wanted to do now was write.

I stormed up the steps to my room and packed. It only took me a few minutes. I left the Christmas presents on the bed. The staff could have them, or maybe they'd give them to Goodwill. They needed them much more than Tegan. I also left the flowers for the staff along with a fifty euro note to thank them for all of their help and kindness.

I pulled my suitcase out the door of my room for the very last time. I made it down the two flights of steps, then to the Beast that waited for me. I looked at my Tissot. It was late: past 1:00 a.m. I started the pickup and engaged the transmission. As I pulled away, I didn't even bother to look back.

Making it to the end of the town, I again glanced at the watch and did some quick calculating: if I kept driving, I'd be home in Eyeries in time for breakfast.

As I turned right down the road that would lead me to Waterville and Sneem, I gunned it. My final thought was that I'd never again visit Portmagee or the Ring of Kerry. For this old man, the memories are too bitter. Besides, now clean and sober, I have the rest of my life to live and other relationships to repair.

You know what? I wouldn't change things for the world.

The End

Trust

By Catherine Ratcliffe A Series of Poems

Mind Over Matter

I must stop thinking
"I love you" so hard.
It's starting to show in my footsteps.

Bandages and Broken Dreams

Sometimes
I wish I were
A child again
Skinned knees are easier
To fix than
A broken heart.

In Universe

If I could know the reason
Behind one single molecule
Of air, gas, cloud, bird,
Winter morning or moon and planets
Gliding through my hat

I could settle myself and say

I am here. The ghost of my ghost
Dances joyously upon a silver rim
That has no beginning or end
Or balance or gravity,
Yet it moves and tips its cup
Of blue rain into a void, departing
If I could understand.

PRELUDE

A rearrangement of clouds
To cover the sky
Is just a prelude
To the grand opening of the sun.

TRUST

There is a shoe in the corner
Is it yours?
It's traveled far, and I can see you walking
From Seattle to Miami
Written on the sole.
Where is your soul?
With me?
Well then,
What of that hole there?
Where did you leave that fraction of yourself?

> *Joy is opening your heart and*
>
> letting it laugh out loud

Insecurity

Within myself
I hear a voice that keeps saying
Break away!
But I think I'll wait until tomorrow.

Gamble

I made a bet with you
That I could love you
Forever.
I lost.
It was longer than that.

Awe

Until comet trails are
Cultivated
In window boxes,
And Saturn's rings are
Wedding bands
Sleep with teddy bear wonder and
Rise in
Barefooted
Birthday anticipation.

The Wedding

Flowing
She unbinds her hair,
The sun spins it into yellow golden silk.
Softly
comes the melody of the morning,
Floating across the fields.
Trusting
She tells her secrets to the butterflies
as they journey through the flowers.

Glowing.
Her hair unfading
as the white dress she wears.
Peaceful.
The air that bathes her, though
Mist surrounds a nearby steeple.
Memories.
Her childhood of freedom drifts through her mind's sky,
Velvet days spread across her vision.
Harshly.
Silver chimes pierce the soft dreams of youth
Scattered as leaves before winter wind.

These poems were written by Catherine for Tom Richards in October 1975 for my birthday, all in Livermore, California. At the time, we were engaged to be married but were too young (or at least I was) to go through with it. Cathy went on to do her law degree at Berkeley. Now living in California, she is so very happy.

Midleton—Through the Memory Mists of 70 Years An Ait Fado

By Thomas Luke Haughton
Edited by Mary Rose Collins

Well, do I remember the little lodge (my childhood home) inside the big red gates of "The Grange" at Midleton, with stone pillars and a big stone ball on top of each. The soughing of the wind through the tops of the tall trees outside my bedroom window, where I slept with my brothers Paddy and Jimmy, acted as a lullaby and wafted us off to sleep. When the night was cold and the rain belted against the window panes, how nice it was to snuggle down together, and we thought of our uncle who was a sailor, and we prayed for him that he might be saved from the perils of the deep.

My father was the gardener at the Big House. We were poor, but looking back, we seem to have always been happy. We had no luxuries which are accepted as normal now. We did not even have running water indoors, merely a tap in the yard—and the toilet was out in the back. It was a terrifying experience going there on a winter's night with a candle to show you the way.

HAVEN OF REST

The lodge, covered in Virginia creeper, was a nice little house with flower beds around two sides and had a porch of latticework and a half door in front, and nearby was a rustic seat surrounded by pink escallonia shrubs. The laburnum trees, when in blossom, made the whole place look sweet and peaceful—a haven of rest. Sheltering the tennis court was a cluster of pampas grass and palm trees, and there were even a few eucalyptus and blue gum trees. The sides of the avenue were lined with beeches in which the rooks built their nests and set up a continuous cawing in early summer. The staff of the Big House included two gardeners, a coachman, and a young lad who drove the pony and trap and worked in the harness room; in the coach house were many types of carriages, a phaeton, a 4-wheeled coach, and a brougham amongst them. At the other side of the stable yard was the coachman's house—always referred to as "Murphy's house"—and the stables.

The domestic staff, which was very rigid in its discipline, was governed by the cook—and, oh, how that kitchen sparkled. The pots and pans shone like mirrors, and the copper ones looked like gold in the reflected light from the ever-glowing fire. The stove itself was a thing of beauty, burnished daily by the scullery maid. There were several maids—parlor maid, house maid, kitchen maid, lady's maid—and a lady's companion for the mistress. All of them worked hard from early morning to late at night for what would be considered a pittance today, but, nevertheless, they were always happy, laughing and singing when out of sight of the gentry.

They were well-dressed and neat, tidy and smart in appearance, a contrast to what they would have been if they had remained in their own little cottages where life was very frugal.

THE CHRISTMAS PARTY

At Christmastime each year, a children's party was held in the Town Hall for all the children of the estate, plus the children of the police and the post office workers. This was a great event, as everyone got a present off the Christmas tree.

There were dolls of all kinds, cradles, and skipping ropes for the girls, and for the boys, there were bugles and drums and little horses with wheels, and some of them even had a butt attached.

The children stuffed themselves with cakes and lemonade and played games such as "Ring-a-Ring-a-Rosie" and "How many miles from this to Dublin?" Afterward, satiated with good food, tired, and happy, they gave "Three cheers for Lord Midleton," who had provided this feast, and wended their weary way home.

At home, Christmas was a great event. The kitchen was decorated with holly and ivy draped around the pictures and on the mantelpiece.

The centerpiece was the Christmas candle. This was a very large candle fixed in a vase or jar and placed on the window ledge. It was decorated with sprigs of variegated holly, and on Christmas Eve, the youngest of the family was lifted up by Father to light it, and there it remained alight all through the festive season. After the lighting of the candle, Father went off to Midnight Mass whilst we trundled off to bed to wait anxiously to see what Father Christmas would bring us in the morning. We, as a family in the lodge, fared well at Christmas. Father got a pound plus a suit of clothes from the master, and then every member of the family at the Big House brought individual presents for my father and mother. Father was always well stocked with pipes and tobacco, as each of the sons (and there were four) would bring him a new pipe and tobacco, and Miss Nesta, the daughter, was also very thoughtful and gave us some groceries. We, the young ones, were not forgotten, and we usually got toy horses for the boys and dolls for our sisters.

The master's sister was a dear old lady. She, unlike the rest of the family, was a Catholic. She lived in Cobh and was known as Miss Geraldine, and she was the author of several books, one notable one being "The Silver Whistle." She generally looked like a "bundle of old clothes," and when local lads saw her coming from the station with a load of "spheres and tattlers" under her arm, they rushed madly to the lodge gate, as she always gave a penny to the lucky one who opened it for her. Many scuffles took place for the honor of being a good Samaritan!

In the summer, how good it felt when, barefooted, we padded in the soft flour-like dust of the road. In those days the dust felt grand as it went between our toes. Sometimes the watering cart for laying the dust would come along. It was a big horse-drawn tank of water with a sprinkler device at the back. It was great fun to run behind it and feel the lovely fresh, clean water on our hot feet—just like balm in Gilead.

OUR COMPANIONS!

During the summer in those far-off days, the sun always seemed to shine brightly in the sky all day and every day, and we wore no boots except on Sundays and when we went back to school. The stepping stones across the river were a source of great fun for us. Some of the stones were a bit wobbly at times, and we often fell in, but it didn't matter as we soon dried out in the sun. I remember one day we were playing there, and two young girls who were the daughters of the Protestant school teacher had joined in with us. Their mother, poor woman, had pretensions of grandeur, and when she came along looking for her chicks, she cried out in horror:

"Oh, what a place, and in such company!" This was a great shock to my brothers and me, as we were very proud of having an uncle who was headmaster in Passage and another who was a petty officer in the Royal Navy—but we were Catholics, hence the different attitude at that time.

A GREAT TEMPTATION

Money was very scarce, and a penny was a "godsend" in those days. One day when running home up the old *boreen*, the white chalky dust oozing through my toes, I spotted a 10s note. I picked it up and jumped over the wall and across the field and gave it to my mother, poor woman!

I think it was about half of my father's weekly wage. It was a great temptation, but she took it right up to the parish priest to have an announcement made from the pulpit on Sunday, and sure enough, Mrs. O'Brien joyfully claimed it and gave me a three-penny bit as a reward for finding it—much to my joy.

Another day I was in luck also as Paddy Goldspring jumped off the back of a hunter outside Fitzgibbons Pub and asked me to hold the horse for him whilst he went in to quench his thirst. It seemed a huge animal, and every time it jerked its head, it nearly had me off my feet. Paddy was a long time in the pub, as it was a hot and dusty day, and when he came out, he gave me a *lop*, and I felt I was "on the pig's back."

WITHOUT A NOD

When I was about seven years old, my poor mother, God rest her soul, was always ailing. I expect life was too tough for her, bringing up six children on a very small wage. She was sick in bed one day, all the others were out, and I was alone with her, and she sang to me, "Oh dear, what can the matter be, Johnny's so long at the fair."

She had a good voice, and I enjoyed hearing her sing, but it brought a lump to my throat and tears to my eyes. Just then I heard the shout of, "Gate." This was the usual signal when someone wanted the gates opened to come into the Big House. It was raining heavily and very cold, and I ran out and opened up the two gates, which wasn't easy, as the gates were heavy. In came the pony and trap, with one of the family and Jack Barry, the coachman, both well wrapped up against the elements, and without a word or a nod, they drove up the tree-lined avenue to the Big House.

I shut the gates and thought to myself how unfair the whole world seemed to be.

"DARKIE"

There was a pathetic little woman well-known in Midleton in those days. She was called "Darkie" and was the widow of a local soldier who had married her in India. Her husband died and left her destitute in an alien land, and she became, in time, a kind of "Sarah Gamp." Her job was to accompany the fever van when collecting cases for the local fever hospital, and also for the poor house. This van was a dismal, black, enclosed coach drawn by a feeble old "head down" horse, and the driver sat on a box seat on top dressed in black and wore a hard hat. Darkie was a tiny, wizened, poor creature who spoke very little English, and her life must have been very miserable, as she hated the climate and had nothing in common with the local people. The only contact she had with them was taking them to the fever hospital to die, which in those days was a very common occurrence. To her great credit, in spite of all her difficulties, she reared a daughter whom she could be proud of.

After the school holidays, it was boots on and away to school. How the bitter cold and the rain came, and I plodded my way down through the "Walks" and across the boggy low field and over the little wooden bridge by the gasworks. One morning at about five minutes to nine, I was making my way swiftly along. The rain was blowing slantwise from the sea, and it was bitterly cold. My shoes, alas, were not of the best and in no time were wet and frozen, and my nose was dripping. I hurried along, as it was getting late, and I had to be there by nine o'clock. "I wish to God," I said, "that I had a good strong pair of boots like Jack McCarthy," but I knew it was wishful thinking, as there were many mouths to be filled at home from a very small budget. So there and then I decided to make a novena to St. Patrick, as his feast day was not far off, and he might help. I could do the novena by the 17th of March if I started now. Well, in spite of my hurrying, I was ten minutes late when I got to school, and on my cold and numb hands, I got three hard whacks from the master with the leather. My hands were numb from the cold, barely felt the pain, but after a while, when the blood began to circulate, I felt the mad tingling and pain, which lasted for about an hour.

After morning prayers, I settled down next to my chum Frankeen and started on the chore of learning what we thought was an awful lot of old *rawmaish*. At the midday break, we went to the playground behind the school and chased a ball around to keep warm. Some of the lucky lads had good solid sandwiches for their break, but most of us had to wait until we got home to break our fast. After the break for play, there was an hour presided over by the headmaster, and he instructed us on table manners and etiquette, how to hold our knife and fork, and how to address our hostess when invited out to dine. We thought to ourselves, "A fat lot of chance we have of ever being in such a situation!"

BACK FROM THE SEA

A few evenings later, who should come into our house but Johnny Mack, a sailor home on leave. I had seen him earlier in the day coming from the railway station with his bundle tied up in a checked handkerchief as was the custom with sailors. How I envied him in his nice uniform and nice, clean, shiny boots. He had three white stripes on his collar, which he told us were to commemorate Nelson's three great victories— Copenhagen, the Nile, and Trafalgar. Johnny pulled out a wallet and showed some wonderful pictures of far and distant lands that he had just returned from—Africa, Suez, Colombo, the Gilbert Isles. The names rolled off his tongue like a babbling stream, and it brought visions of sunshine and brightness and smiles and sandy beaches in vivid contrast to the rain and wind howling outside. I sat spellbound, absorbed in it all, and I could hardly sleep that night thinking of it. I pictured myself like Jim Hawkins of *Treasure Island,* going to those wonderful sunlit lands of tall coconut palms and date palms and the nice brown friendly people. There was even a place called the Friendly Islands, Johnny had said, and I promised myself that I, too, would see these wonderful lands one day. Which I eventually did—fifty years later,

About this time, we used to hear the grown-ups talking about events in Europe and that the Germans were planning to go to war with England. As there were quite a few men around who were army and naval reservists, they had a personal interest in this. Shortly after the night of Johnny's visit, a friend, May Ingham, came up as usual for the milk, and we could see that she had been crying. When my mother asked her what was the matter, she said that her father, who was an army reservist, had been called up. Poor May never saw her dad again, as he was killed in action in France. Johnny Mack, of course, had to return to his ship at once, and he was fortunate enough to return after the war.

There was great enthusiasm in those early days of that First World War. The lads who for years had not had a decent coat to their backs now strutted about in their khaki uniforms. The proudest ones were the cavalry and horse regiments like the South Irish Horse. How they swanked with their jingling spurs and a crop under their arms as they walked around the town, admired by the girls and the small boys. I remember well one Sunday morning going into Bridgie Ahern's for a pennyworth of bullseyes. Larry Keating came in. He was a very smart-looking horse soldier, with spurs and a crop, and a leather bandolier around him. He called for a packet of woodbines and put his tuppence on the counter. "I'm off to France tomorrow, Bridgie," he said, "and we will soon have them German buggars on the run." Poor Larry, he was only sixteen years old, and before another Sunday was out, he was blown to pieces near La Bassee Road in France.

The first member of the Irish National Volunteers to go was a drapers clerk in town, and he was escorted to the station by the fife and drum band and numerous townspeople who cheered him and wished him Godspeed. He never returned either.

I remember sometime before these events, we used to play around the gas lamp in the winter evenings, after it was lit by Billy Reilly with his long pole. One evening some of the big lads pretended to hang "Daisy" Cashman from the crossarm of the gas lamp, and a few months after this event, poor Daisy died in the mud of Flanders.

In the Old Cork Road during that dreadful period of 1914 to 1918, there were sad homesteads. Many of the lads left never to return. If I remember correctly, there were twenty-one houses on that road, and out of that number, there were twenty-five men in the army and navy.

Of the four sons of the "Big House" (Penrose Fitzgerald), two were killed. There were Lieutenant Mulhall, killed in action; two Cotters in the Munsters; Steve Leary, killed in the Battle of Jutland, his brother Paddy in the RHA; Simon Sellers and his brother in the Munsters; Pat Hallisey of the Munsters lost a leg; Johnny McCarthy; Paddy Goldspring; and "Daisy."

Cashman and his stepbrother were both killed in action, and their father, Pat.

Also killed in action were: Mick Sheehan, RE; Jerome and Henry Coughlan, Henry killed in action; Lynch R. N. died; Mick McEvoy, who was only a schoolboy in the RIR, and May Ingham's father was killed in action. They left in their prime, and many left their bones to fertilize the crops of Flanders, and some went to Davy Jones's Locker. May they all rest in peace.

MICHAEL COLLINS

Michael Collins was, in my opinion, the most outstanding Irishman of his generation. He was born in 1890 in a little hamlet between Clonakilty and Rosscarbery called Sam's Cross. The Collins family had a Public House there for several generations, and I think they are still there. These were cousins of Michael's parents. His father bore the same name, and his mother was Mary Ann O'Brien. Michael was the eighth child of the family and was born when his father was actually aged seventy-five years. The father was an extraordinary man; although a humble farmer, he was well versed in Greek, Latin, and English as well as his native tongue. He also had a reputation as a mathematician; all this knowledge he gained from a hedge schoolmaster, Dermot O'Sullivan, as the Catholic Irish did not have schools in those days.

The great Michael Collins became a pupil at Lisavaird National School and came under the influence of the headmaster, Denis Lyons, who wrote of him that he was "exceptionally intelligent, a good reader, and had a striking interest in Irish history, politics, and engineering. A good sportsman though temperamental."

Later at Clonakilty School, he studied for the civil service and lived with his sister, who was a Mrs. O'Driscoll, whose husband was the editor of the local paper. Young Michael helped in this work by doing a bit of journalism, reporting local events.

Later, having passed his examination for the civil service, he was posted to the Post Office Savings Bank, West Kensington, London, and during his period there, he stayed at No. 5 Netherwood Place, West Kensington. Whilst in London, he joined the Irish Republican Brotherhood, and this started him on the road that eventually led to his place in the Hall of Fame of his country and to his death in his country's cause.

He returned to Ireland and participated in the Easter Rising in Dublin. He was staff captain and ADC to Joseph Plunkett in the GPO. Taken prisoner, he was interned in Wales. After his release in 1918, he was elected a Sinn Féin member of the Dáil, which was a government in name only, as Ireland was at that time still under English rule. In 1921 he and Arthur Griffiths were mainly responsible for the final treaty with the British Government, which gave Ireland the status of a self-governing country similar to Australia and Canada. This was called the Irish Free State. This satisfied most of the people of Ireland at the time, as they were tired of the years of bloodshed during the Black and Tan troubles. There were others, however, such as De Valera, Cathal Bruga, Liam Lynch, etc., who did not agree, and they took up arms against the new state and thus started the Irish Civil War.

Michael Collins took command of the Free State Army, and a lot of others in the previous fight against the British also became Free Staters. After many bloody fights, he crushed the opposition in Dublin, Limerick, and all the large towns and eventually came around by sea and made a landing at Kinsale and captured it. It was at this time that

General Collins (as he then was) decided to do a tour of inspection of Cork and District in August. He made a trip down to Sam's Cross to see his homestead, or the site of it, as it had been destroyed by the Black and Tans. He was received with rapture by the people of the locality, and he bought a round of drinks of the famous Clonakilty "Wrestler" for all that were with him. Later that day, they set out to return to Cork City. The convoy with him consisted of a motorcycle scout in front, followed by a Crossley tender containing two officers, eight men, and two Lewis gunners. General Collins himself and major general Emmett Dalton (who now lives in Kent, 1979) were next in a Leyland Touring car with two drivers, Corry and Quinn. Bringing up the rear was a small, armored car called the "Slievenamom," which was in the charge of a Scotsman named McPeake. Their route was via Skibbereen and Bandon, and when they came to the valley of Béal na Bláth, which is northwest of Bandon, on rounding a bend, they found the road obstructed by a brewer's dray overturned and crates and bottles strewn all over the road. It was evening, and the light was fading; all at once, intense fire from rifles and machine guns was opened on them from across the valley. The road they were on was very exposed and had little cover. General Collins gave the order to get out, take cover and return the fire. He with Emmett Dalton lay down behind a small bank and opened fire. Dalton called on the armored car to fire, but McPeake said that the gun was jammed. The firing died away, and after a while, Collins got up to have a good look to see what was happening. He stood on the road, looking to where the firing had been coming from and reloading his rifle. A single shot rang out and thus ended the life of a brave and noble Irishman who will never be forgotten.

This unhappy event happened on August 22, 1922. I was a young lad aged sixteen years at the time and was a member of the Free State Army.

Thomas L. Haughton, published in *Cork Holly Bough*, 1979

(edited by Mary Rose Collins, 2022)

boreen: small unpaved pathlop: a penny
rawmaish: foolish talk

About the Author

Thomas Luke Haughton (1904–1992) (my father) was born in Cobh / County Cork. The story is made of his memories as a child and young man in Ireland, written seventy years later. They are vivid and evocative, showing something of his spirit and optimism as a child. Times were tough, but they still had fun.

It is poignant in its references to war and death. However, he makes no reference to the deaths of his younger brothers, Jimmy and Paddy, who died within a month of each other when Dad was only seven years old. I can only imagine that this must have cut very deep. I have no memory of him ever talking about them, although they are referred to in the story, accompanied by happy memories.

At the end of the story, he tells us he joined the Free State Army. After that, my family is unclear as to what happened, though it has been suggested that he needed to leave Ireland, as members of the IRA were looking for him. He came to England and joined the Royal Navy; he was stationed in Plymouth. The Royal Navy gave him the opportunity to travel and see some of the far-off places he had heard about as a child. He became a sick berth attendant, qualifying on April 5, 1927. When seeing his certificate, my mother was amused to see that he passed all subjects as good or very good, apart from one. Cooking for the sick was marked "fair." She always said he couldn't even boil an egg!

Tom married my mother, Connie Carey, in 1936, in Plymouth. My brother Patrick was born there in 1942. My sister Sheenagh was born in 1948. Tom developed his medical knowledge to become a pharmacist, and the family moved to Barnstaple in North Devon, where I was born.

Tom worked in the local doctors' surgery until he retired. He was very knowledgeable regarding diagnosis, but still couldn't cook!

As a child and young woman, I did not relate well to Tom. I look back on it now and wonder why. He was a kind man, very sociable and friendly, but communication between us could be strained. I think his early life must have left scars that we were unaware of. He had become the youngest child at age seven with three older sisters who I believe doted on him. I wonder what effect that had on him.

Rereading his story, I reflected on times when I had been annoyed with him when he had taken my three young sons down to the local Devon *boreen*, bringing them back wet and dirty from playing in the river. I saw the parallel with his escapades with his brothers and realized he was possibly reliving those times with his grandsons. I feel sorry now that I was harsh with him, but I was a young mother with my own ideas on parenting.

In their retirement years, Tom and Connie lived in Braunton, North Devon. They both had twenty-plus years to enjoy retirement. For Tom, that meant long walks, golf, reading and painting, and generally a nap in the afternoon. He was also interested in genealogy, an interest which I have also developed in recent years.

Mary Rose Collins March 2022

Strangers & Closeness: A Collection of Poems
by Larry Wilson

A Sonnet in February
I could believe, were I believing kind
that time and fate conspired to make us one
a clever strategy, conspiracy
of spirit, sneaky mystery of lust
and harmony, combining in a love
surprising everyone who sees its glow
but fate, however smug, must fall behind
and wait its turn for credit. What we've done
is more than marriage, more than constancy
and harder, far, than others see it. Just
as planets orbits stars, the physics of
our love is more complex than people know
to call it "fate" is shorthand, nothing more
for wordless knowledge from the heart's bright core

Halfway Home
it's never been a question of the choice
of what to say, but rather where to start—
with childhood? with birth? That's so cliché
and at the halfway mark of life, I thirst
for something unexpected, something sure

to corkscrew all that's come and gone before

so patience with me while I find my voice
my pen, my wineglass, while I probe my heart
with needle tip of honesty. The way
to tell the truth is not to cry the worst
alone, and not to hold the best as pure
but claim both sun and shadow, peace and war

may dawn and nightfall dance between my rhymes
and candor grant me distance, grace, and time

Strange Day

a strange day—warm as summer, but no leaves
on any trees. I cannot say I like
the neighbors watching me, in bare feet, shirt-
less, digging in the garden, eating bread
and cheese on patio ("They're drinking wine
at half-past twelve on Sunday afternoon?")

but warmth like this is benison, and even
if the chill returns, today I'm psyched
for springtime, ready for the garden work
the lawn to mow, the weedy flower beds
I'm ready for the lazy evening times
on porch or pergola. Pray, goddess, soon

and no more days below the freezing mark
set free the silken breezes after dark

Close

what if the concrete curb there, fifty feet
away, beyond the roses and the lawn,
were waterline, uneven stair of stone,
        descending to a bright and lively sea?
what if, whenever fancy took my heart,

I could abandon daily household chores
and take a path that leads to seashore, not
    suburban street and neighbors' driveways, homes?
instead of oaks and elms, I'd see a field
of hardy grasses rippling in a stiff
and salty wind, the sky so blue it stings
    the eye, and blue beyond, horizons wide

This twilight, close the eyes and dream a dream
of island shores, as close as memory

Delivery Pending

you wouldn't think so small a living room
would echo, but it does, with so much furn-
iture removed. The sofas coming in
a week or so, a sleek armchair, a bench
and there's a brand-new carpet to be laid
an antique bookcase, brighter reading lights

we've been here just four years—no, not too soon
to think redecoration. We have learned
the way the sunlight falls on frigid winter days, the summer breezes paths, the wrench
of certain doorknobs. Knowing that we'll stay
awhile, suddenly we itch to right

the wrongs our glad enthusiasm wrought
those lovely, frantic days when first we bought

Critique

"This isn't poetry, it's narrative,"
he said. "You need to add some metaphors

and similes, and make it more abstract.
You're not describing anything, you're just
relating incidents, and I, for one,
want something more when I pick up a poem."

"But this is how I work and how I live,"
I told him, "how I seek a pattern for
the shifting fractals and the random acts.
It's all about accumulation. Must
a writer only, always do what's done
already? Is the genre carved in stone?"

"It's dull," he said. "It isn't verse to me."
"It's verse," I told him, "theoretically."

Begin with an Ending

Alone, with lilies, candles. Horrible:
A wooden coffin, and the girl within—
No, not a girl—no, that's the history
That binds me, blinds me. No, a *woman* dead
My sister, thirty-five, two children left
Behind, a husband (sullen, lumpy troll)

Who, nonetheless, did cry, his belly full
Of beer. My mother shattered, quenched, convinced
This death must somehow be her fault, that she
Had failed her daughter somehow. Eyes cracked red
With grief, my brothers mute with shock, bereft
And angry. Lucky me—I had a whole

Half hour to myself, alone, before
The hordes arrived, to make my peace with her

An Experienced Eye

there always comes a day—it's late this year—
when I can look up at the backyard oak
and count the few remaining leaves in their
entirety. Sometimes I'm raking, sometimes banking roses; this year merely walking
to the garage. Today's the day. The fall

"officially"   is   over.   Cold   draws   near
it's breathing down my neck, the autumn cloak
of color withers, shreds; the winds will tear
my warmth away, the sun goes weak, and come
the dark, it might as well be winter. Chalk
it up to forty years of counting all

the leaves remaining on November trees:
see?—only twelve. Tomorrow comes the freeze

In Photographs
it's not that I'm ashamed, though shame is part
of it. I don't want anyone to think
we had no happy times, though we were poor
and Mom and Dad worked very hard to give
us food and shelter, clothes and Christmas toys—
but still this shadow-pain: it could have been

so much a better childhood. My heart
insists on honesty, where memory shrinks
and tries to hide the truth: my brothers were
a nasty lot, my father hard to live
with, mother an enabler of the boys'
inherent selfish violence. The sin

comes not in naming it, but in the half-
truths, as we pose so sweet for photographs

Turning My Back on the Wind

in dreams, I turn my back upon the wind
and spread my fingers wide to feel the sails
unfurl, unseen, then leaning, trusting, all
at once I cabriole and I am in
the air, a kite, a drifting breath, a bird
a dancing leaf, unbound by gravity

some people tell me flight in dreams has been
interpreted as sexual denial:
anytime I leap but do not fall
I'm sublimating lust, replacing sin
with purified angelic pleasure. Words
of weighty scholarship, no doubt, but we

know better, we who turn our backs upon
the wind, and let it lift us high, beyond

Pussy Willow

twelve years old, a February wander
in farm fields gone to wastelands
soon to be housing estates

I found a pussy willow tree
growing in a muddy, flooded ditch
catkins just showing silver against blue sky

snapped off a slender branch, hurried home
filled an old blue Mason jar with water
slowly, slowly, I watched it grow white roots

then green leaves. In April I planted it
in that corner of the garden I claimed as mine
taller every year. A fine tree. Elegant

but they don't often live long, pussy willows
two decades later, weakened with canker
it fell in a fierce winter windstorm

I didn't know. I'd moved away by then
my father cut it up for firewood
before I could salvage a branch for rooting

it was a tree that could have gone on
a long, long time, parent to child
silver soft against every blue springtime

A Rose Catalogue

a rose catalog in the post today
pure flower porn, all color and promises
imagine an avenue of bright yellow, softest amber
the way the scent rises like rich summer perfume

we won't be buying any, probably
there are sixteen bushes in the garden already
bright against the bricks, arching on the pergolas
dreams of more can stay just dreams

but we don't have a purplish one, do we
and there isn't a true red, just pinks in all tones
from baby's cheeks to apricot to flushed copper
we won't buy more—but we could. We always could

Plum

there's a plum tree on the riverbank

strong, deep-rooted, wind-twisted
I've never seen fruit on its branches
but every year it bravely blossoms

flowers faintly pink, almost white, delicate
like something out of a Japanese woodblock print
a corona of stamens, inquisitive cat whiskers
a scent that's a promise of warmer days

not sure how it grew here, or why
there are no other plum trees anywhere near
the damson in my garden isn't blooming yet
or I'd cut a branch and leave it there in a jar

to see if the bees might cross-pollinate
to cross fingers for wild plums next summer
to scatter their stones all along the river
to imagine a future froth of springtime bloom

Not at Rest

five hundred years ago, my father's folk
were kings in Ireland. Beside a lake
in green and northern hills, a thornbush bloomed
above the crowning stone, and choirs sang
in Latin and in Gaelic. Swords were bright
and harps were strung with singing silver wire

the folk today are scattered, names forgot
the bloodline thinned by distance, torn by war
and no one prays at Lisnaskea for
the wisdom of the dead to bless their rule
still two or three in every generation
hear the echoes of the singing harp

and keep alive a vision of a past
so long ago, so far, and not at rest

Tweed

an elegant bottle of perfume, an old one
sacred on my mother's dresser
I knew the word—"Tweed"
but I thought it just meant an itchy fabric

the smell was lovely, strange (oranges? violets?)
although I was told time and again
to leave it alone—expensive stuff
and perfume was only for ladies

then one day in school, the art teacher
taught us to twist roses out of colored tissue
tie them to pipe cleaner stems
simple green leaves cut with pinking shears

I was fascinated. I must have made a dozen
and then she suggested a finesse—
dab a small cotton ball with perfume
and tuck one inside each paper rose

by the time I was finished, the Tweed bottle
was almost empty, and Mom couldn't be mad
because I gave most of the bouquet to her
one single rose to Gran, and one to Aunt Marian

who gave me a big kiss and announced (loudly)
to everyone at dinner that I had very good taste
for a seven-year-old, that Tweed was her favorite
that it was a beautiful rose, and wasn't I a clever boy

Guides

the robin follows me around the garden
impatient for the soil to be turned
to catch the worm

the blackbird perched on wire, bright eye glinting
a liquid trill of song, a sonic drug—
he eats a bug

quartet of ducks, in tight formation flying
steep curving dive, harsh quacks like barking dogs
they're death to frogs

observe the tits, the thrushes, noble herons
the bating sparrowhawks, the darting swifts
I wonder if

our feathered friends could use a handy guidebook
describing types of people they might see
humanity

in all its shapes and sizes and behaviors
the types most likely to provide, in need
fat worms, birdseed

Ordinary Day
warm afternoon, now cooling away
snapping winds going evening-soft
birdsong still loud as Wagnerian divas
and were starting to think about dinner

weeds cleared, petunias planted
squishing green spittlebugs on the lavender
a chat with friends over their garden gate
and definitely thinking about dinner

nothing in the post today (so what?)
but electric messages from friends around the world

preparing a fire in the chiminea
and selecting the spices and green herbs for dinner

an ordinary day in a world gone extraordinary
a quiet day in a world that can be too shrill
a simple day when so many have been complicated
and dinner, when we get that far, will be delicious

House

the house isn't there anymore
torn down for a hospital carpark
the house they struggled, early on
to pay the mortgage for
the house they raised five children in
it isn't there anymore

which can't be true, can it?
back door key still on memory's ring
I know exactly how high on the wall
the kitchen light switch is
I know which stair treads creak
        and how many steps it is
        to what was my attic bedroom
        now hanging ghostly in midair
and the careful, quiet slam needed
to close the bathroom door
I know the golden-brown shimmer
of the narrow-boarded oak floors
just after waxing
I know the shade cast by six enormous elm trees
before the blight cut them down
I know the gas light burning 24/7
in the middle of the front lawn
surrounded by tulips, and, later, petunias
the dogs, the cars in the driveway

the garage door so difficult to wrench open
the lilacs in spring, the acre of lawn to mow, grumbling
the enormous vegetable garden in summer
the white ash tree towering, the apples, the cherries
the vast prairie sunsets and the knee-deep winter snow

it can't be true, can it?
but the house isn't there anymore
and that corner of the car park is so remote
that no one ever parks there

so let me build the house in memory's clapboards
a firm foundation and a coat of white paint
        I know that the shutters were blue
        I wonder what happened to them

Wordplay

I play with words
I dance with words
I mess with words
and words mess with me

it's a Möbius strip
it's a Sondheim libretto
it's complicated, it's difficult
it's all I have and all I want

they mesh, they merge
words like DNA molecules
if they're not exact
they're not real. Not true

it's the taste on the tongue
it's the fragrance, the feel
the sandpaper of a cat's tongue
or it is nothing at all

Always Room

there is always room for forgiveness
there is always a way past despair
but it's a hard road, paved with toothy gravel
sharp flints, rusted nails, razor blades
and all of us are barefoot, all of us

there is always room for apology
there is a roadmap toward redemption
but it is drawn in heart's blood
begrudged at times, but burning bright
and all of us are bleeding, all of us

there is always an open sky above
there's a hushed message, a metaphor for hope
but even standing on tiptoe, we cannot reach it
fingertips straining, hoping for clean and empty air
all of us yearning to fly, all of us

About Lawrence Wilson

Lawrence Wilson's fiction, poetry, and essays have appeared in *Albedo One, Agenda, Gramarye, One Hand Clapping, Ink, Sweat and Tears, Three Drops from a Cauldron, Stone, Root and Bone, Best of British, The Poetry of Roses, The Pocket Poetry Book of Marriage, The Pocket Poetry Book of Cricket, and The Darker Side of Love,* on Salon.com, and in other journals and collections. His first three collections, *The April Poems, Another April,* and *An Illustrated April,* are available on Amazon, as is his children's novel, *Mina,* and other writing.
To contact the author above:

Lawrence Wilson
52 Military Road
Rye, East Sussex TN31 7NY

Tom Richards

wilsonlawrenceuk@gmail.com

OPHELIA'S ScRaMbLeD ROYAL EGG

By Pheloneous Egg Esq, Egg Merchant (ghostwritten by Tom Richards, infamous not-so-famous author) A Farce in ONE ACT— thanks Be to God, with profuse apologies to William Shakespeare

Dedicated to:

Ophelia and her five sisters: Edith, Carm, Kris, Liz, and Rose

This play for the stage takes place in the Globe Theatre, London, England and is also reprised at a temporary open-air theatre built especially for this production in Nottingham City, also in England

Time: Merry Old England in the Seventeenth Century

CURTAIN UP

<u>SCENE I: INSIDE THE ROYAL EGG CASTLE, COURTYARD</u>

ALARM! ALARM!
ENTER **MARCELLUS**, ROYAL DANISH SOLDIER AND
SHEILA, ROYAL FOOD PROVISIONER
ALARM! ALARM! AGAIN!!!

Marcellus: But soft, what light through yon window breaks? Is it the east? The west? Or is it the Royal Platform walking so softly on yon window sill, his Highness, Hamlet, THE ROYAL EGG???!
Sheila: (sotto and out of character) That's the wrong play, you loser!
Marcellus: (sotto and also out of character) What's that you say, fair fathead?
Sheila: I'm no fathead! If you don't straighten up your act, I'll beat you senseless with this!

WAPS MARCELLUS ON THE HEAD
WITH A GIANT METAL WHISK.

SFX: B-O-O-O-ING AS MARCELLUS
STAGGERS AND HITS THE DECK

KING EGG HAMLET APPEARS ON HIGH
RAMPARTS ABOVE THEM

BELOW HIM, **OPHELIA** ENTERS ONTO THE MAIN STAGE

Hamlet: 'Tis I, King Egg! Here to take on my rival, the horrible Claudius. But only after I go to the loo. Now, who has the royal golden toilet paper?
KING EGG HAMLET WALKS OFF STAIRS ONTO THE MAIN STAGE
Marcellus: Not I, sire. I use the fragrant leaf of a nearby sycamore tree to wipe my rump. Oh! Is that a piece of Royal Eggshell I see before me?

MARCELLUS PICKS UP A GIANT PIECE OF EGGSHELL

Hamlet: Forsooth! It is me arse that has fallen off! Stick it back on, quick, my good Marcellus, my knight idiot.

MARCELLUS USES A GIANT TUBE OF SUPERGLUE
TO COVER HAMLET'S NAKED ARSE

Hamlet: Oh, there is my fair Ophelia, my future wife, my life!
Ophelia: And there is the egg of my dreams, my champion. (to Marcellus, soto) I want to choke him at the seams.

TRUMPETS SOUND **POLONIUS** ENTERS
FROM CASTLE INTERIOR

Polonius: Is that the fair Claudius I hear?
Ophelia: Oh, that it was not so! My heart is fix-ed on the giant royal eggshell!

ENTER **CLAUDIUS** WITH TALL GUARD **GEORGE**

Claudius: George, you lackey. Where is Hamlet, my sworn enemy?
George: On the toilet, squire, should memory serve me right. I was just on my way to collect the Royal Goldleaf toilet paper when
Hamlet: I am here, Claudius and knave George. Claudius, prepare to defend thy-self!

HAMLET DRAWS HIS STEEL SWORD. HE ADVANCES,
BUT THEN COWERS BEHIND GEORGE.

Hamlet: I must make my royal egg run because it be a Tuesday. I cannot fight ye, you cowardly Claudius.

ENTER HORSE WITH MODERN TRAILER
PILED HIGH WITH EGGS

Hamlet: You see? I am not lying. Now, why do you not bow to me, Claudius?
Claudius: I bow to no one, not even a cracked egg like you. Now, I shall skewer you if you don't allow me a moment with fair Ophelia.

CLAUDIUS POINTS HIS SWORD AT HAMLET.
HAMLET SIDESTEPS, SHAKING WITH FEAR.

Claudius: Oh, fair maiden. Soul of my soul. I would die for you because of the beauty of thy heart. Made all the more beautiful by that light green smock you wear.
Ophelia: Beat it, silly.
Claudius: You would call your true love silly? What, and you would marry Hamlet, my sworn enemy? Oh, Ophelia, I beg ye: let me marry thee!
Ophelia: Scram before I call the cops, ya fecker.

CLAUDIUS PUTS BOTH HANDS ON HIS HEART
AND TURNS TO THE ROYAL EGG HAMLET.

Claudius: The lady doth protest too much.
Hamlet: I told you she had a crush on me. My fair dream loves eggs for breakfast.

MARCELLUS TAKES OPHELIA'S HAND
AND PULLS HER TO A CORNER.

Marcellus: Let not these ruffians sway thy heart, beautiful Ophelia. George, by gum, has given me the note you wrote for me. You have agreed to marry me?
Ophelia: That I have, my prince and liege. But it is secret and tell no one! And I shall seal my troth with a kiss which I shall place upon thy lips.

HAMLET AND CLAUDIUS RUSH TO BREAK THEM
UP AS SHEILA, FOOD PROVIDER, SCREAMS:

Sheila: Dinner's ready! Get it while it's hot, you bunch of idiots.

CURTAIN DOWN, CURTAIN UP

<u>SCENE II: THE ROYAL DINING ROOM</u>

Hamlet: My love, Ophelia. I command ye sit beside me as is my royal egg prerogative.

AS HAMLET AND OPHELIA SIT, CLAUDIUS RUSHES IN AND PUSHES OVER HAMLET. THE EGG CRACKS AGAIN. KING EGG HAMLET BENDS TO MARCELLUS, SITTING NEAR.

Hamlet: This time, my dear Marcellus, do not apply the superglue as you did before. Let them think that I am mad, and in my madness, I shall destroy that dastardly Claudius. You are true blue and trustworthy, are you not? You will help me win Ophelia's hand, and for Claudius, that will be my parting shot.

Marcellus: (winking at Ophelia as he rises and bows) Yes, my royal eggshell arse. If it is your will, then you shall be well done.

TRUMPETS SOUND. ENTER A GIANT
THREE-HEADED KANGAROO.

THE SISTERS, **CIARA**, **SANDRA ONE** AND **SANDRA TWO**
CONSTANTLY KNOCK THEIR THREE HEADS TOGETHER.

Ciara: (gazing at Hamlet) Look, sisters, but who do I spy!

Sandra Two: (gazing at Marcellus) Why he is the fairest fairy in all the land.

Sandra One: (gazing at Ophelia) Like a gorgeous swan with chickenpox.

Ciara: Oh, my heart breaks because my love knows not that I love him!

Sandra One: (continuing on about Ophelia) Like a spring day outing, with a vivid complexion.

Sandra Two: Oh, my darling, my lover, my future partner.

Ciara: My Hamlet.

Sandra Two: My Marcellus.

Sandra One: My Ophelia.

THE TWO SISTERS LOOK ASKANCE AT SANDRA ONE.

Ciara: I never knew you swung that way, Sandy, my sister.
Sandra One: Hey, whichever way the wind blows is fine by me.

THE THREE HEADS NOD IN AGREEMENT.
ENTER POLONIUS

Polonius: Daughter, I have heard that ye have betrothed yourself to young Marcellus!

SANDRA TWO FAINTS. THE ENTIRE KANGAROO STAGGERS.

Ophelia: Father, be quiet. Don't you know 'tis a secret.
Hamlet: Hold now, ye wench! Am I right to hear that you are in love with Marcellus!
Marcellus: And so it is true, my royal egg. I would die for her, but even if you love us,
know that my life will have been lived in vain if I do not have the hand of sweet Ophelia, my snuggle-puss.
Claudius: Sound the alarm! For I shall invade this kingdom with troops loyal to me.
Oh, Marcellus, ye be a dead man. Oh, King Egg Hamlet, ye shall be fried on a plate just for me. And as for you, you Kangaroos! Go back to Australia and to your zoo!
Ophelia: Do I not have a say in the matter? I am Ophelia, not a slave. I am in love with Marcellus, and so it shall be that no man or eggshell shall sunder what God has meant for me.
Hamlet/Claudius: Quiet, you jam jar! You gave your hand to me!
Ophelia: (shrugs) So what?
Marcellus: There is only one way to sort this out, and you both know what I mean
Hamlet: A duel
Claudius: A duel!
Polonius: Yes, but there have to be two dual'ers, not three, because that's what a dual is. One on one, not three on three. So now, let's stage it quickly while the fates are with us, especially me.

POLONIUS BOWS TO THE AUDIENCE.
CURTAIN DOWN, CURTAIN UP

SCENE III: JOUSTING AREA HAMLET,
CLAUDIUS, AND MARCELLUS APPEAR WITH
LLOONNGGG JOUSTING SPEARS.

Hamlet: But should we not fight with daggers? This spear makes me stagger.

Claudius: Though this be madness, there is method to it. Much better than a large dagger.

The Kangaroo including Sandra One, Sandra Two, and Ciara: Give them to us! Thirty feet of spear is much better than six inches of hot dagger!

SANDRA ONE WINKS AT HER SISTERS.

Sandra One: If you know what I mean.

Sheila Food Provisioner: (aside to Ophelia) Would it not be better to, in the earth, plant our King Hamlet Egg? The fertilizer he would make t'would be good for lettuce with wine vinaigrette, a perfect lunch!

ALARM! ALARM! GEORGE RUNS IN

George: It neareth midday, my king and liege. Have you forgotten about the egg delivery? I've spent all day giving your trailer a a new livery!

THE EGG TRAILER IS PULLED OUT, PAINTED BRIGHT
PINK, STILL FULL OF OLD EGGS. POLONIUS AND
SHEILA SWOON TO THE FLOOR FROM THE STINK.

Hamlet: (infuriated) Something is rotten in the state of Denmark. My words fly up, my thoughts remain below; words without thought never to heaven go!

Ophelia: Is that a rotten egg I smell, or could that be you, you king, you fool.

Hamlet: 'Tis not me, I swear!

Claudius: 'Tis you, dear King. I'm trading in my spear for a dagger deep! George! My dagger.

GEORGE MAKES A BIG DEAL OF WALKING
COMPLETELY AROUND THE STAGE, INTENT
ON IMPRESSING CLAUDIUS. MEANWHILE
OPHELIA UNWRAPS A CEREMONIAL BLACK CLOTH,
REVEALING THREE DAGGERS. SHE DIPS ONE IN A PAIL
MARKED WITH A LARGE LABEL: POISON! BEWARE!

Marcellus: Are you certain this will work?

Ophelia: So I am, I am certain.

Marcellus: But, Ophelia, are they not your daggers? As your father's egg mouth says so eloquently: "Neither a borrower nor a lender be; for loan oft loses both itself and friend, and borrowing dulls the edge of husbandry."

Ophelia: Shut it, Marcellus. Now be quick! Take this one, for upon it is God's vengeance for our lost love. (She gives Marcellus the poisoned dagger.)

GEORGE NOW STANDS IN FRONT OF MARCELLUS.

George: That dagger be the king's, not his daughter's! Give it here, you pig.

GEORGE GRABS THE BLADE AND CUTS HIMSELF.

Ophelia: (horrified) Oh, did the dagger scratch thee, bold George?

George: Ay, ay, a scratch, just a scratch but 'tis enough. Go, Ophelia, fetch a surgeon.

GEORGE STUMBLES.

Marcellus: Courage, man, the hurt cannot be much.

George: No, 'tis not so deep as a well, nor so wide as a church door, nor so large as a kingly boiled egg, but 'tis enough. Twill serve. Ask for me tomorrow, and you shall find me a grave man. I am peppered, and will do to serve my master, King Egg Hamlet.

GEORGE TWIRLS AND FALLS TO THE GROUND, DEAD. THE KANGAROOS SCREAM!

Hamlet: (dazed) Who has killed my loyal George? When I would be done smashing Claudius's head, I would knight fair George as a man having the courage of hot porridge!

Claudius: It was not me! It must have been that treasonous daughter of yours, but my one true love, the fair Ophelia!

Ophelia: Me? Now how could that ever be! Marcellus, I beg you to defend me, and restore my honor which means so much to me.

CLAUDIUS SPIES THE POISON PAIL

Claudius: But look, my royal Hamlet, my kingly egg! Is that a bucket of poisoned blood or a pot to boil your broken arse in?

Marcellus: To arms! Prepare to defend thyself, fair Claudius.

MARCELLUS PULLS HIS DAGGER. THEY FIGHT.

Ophelia: Kill him quick, my fair prince Marcellus. Know that my hand protects your heart, for I will die should Claudius win.

CLAUDIUS WOUNDS MARCELLUS IN THE FACE WITH HIS DAGGER.

Ophelia: O, woe is me. I have seen what I have seen; see what I see!

MARCELLUS FIGHTS BACK. THEY TWIRL, AND CLAUDIUS FINDS A DAGGER THRUST DEEP INTO HIS CHEST.

Claudius: 'Tis done! Now I am a dead man. No longer will I dream of having my cherished Princess Ophelia at my side. Instead, I will rot like a stately, kingly scrambled egg loyal man.

CLAUDIUS KEELS OVER, DEAD.

Polonius: Do you see now, fair Daughter, what your beauty does to men? Due to your betrayal, you have fried not one but two young men?
Ophelia: I have betrayed no one, dear Father, and do trust me. There is not a living couple so loving but that it is Marcellus and me.

SHEILA THE FOOD PROVISIONER STORMS
TO THE CENTER OF THE STAGE.

Sheila: Now take your places, for breakfast is late due to all of this blasted fighting! And, Ophelia, the eggs are all as rotten as is the State of Denmark. Look at the egg truck and smell the stink of its pink! We'll not have scrambled eggs as planned, but instead Danish butter and toast.
Polonius: Therefore, since brevity is the soul of wit, and tediousness the limbs and outward flourishes, I will be brief. I realize that it is not my daughter's fault that those men died, but the cowardly nature of the prince of eggs, King Egg Hamlet!
Hamlet: (cowering behind Sheila) Let no man judge his king, for I be God's own law in this land, the State of Denmark! We shall breakfast and forget this trouble. Now, Cook Sheila. Fry up the toast in Danish butter, for it is one of my favorite things, and I'm all in a lather!

SHEILA BEGINS TO HEAT AN ENORMOUS
FRYING PAN OVER GLOWING CINDERS.

The Kangaroo Sisters (all together): Make lots of toast, dear sister. Fried with Danish butter, it is also one of our favorite things, and the king of eggs does not matter.
Ophelia: Toast be damned. Marcellus, I thought you had promised to defend my honor? Or perhaps it is because you do not love me?

Marcellus: How would you think that of me? Fair King Hamlet, prepare to be drawn and quartered. Your egg center will soon be dust due to the love that you have for my lovely Ophelia.

AGAIN MARCELLUS DRAWS HIS DAGGER. HE
CHASES HAMLET AROUND THE GIANT FRYING
PAN. AT LAST, MARCELLUS CORNERS HIM.

Marcellus: Die, you dog, you coward.

MARCELLUS THRUSTS WITH HIS DAGGER. THE KING
OF EGGS, HAMLET, FALLS INTO THE FRYING PAN.
HIS EGG BODY SMASHES, AND HE BEGINS TO FRY
AS SHEILA STIRS HIM WITH A GIANT SPOON.

Hamlet: (to Ophelia) I'm frying! I'm frying! Oh, look at what you've done to me, you little wench!
Marcellus: Are you satisfied now, Ophelia, for with Hamlet's death, I begin to smell a stench of a royal wench!

SANDRA ONE FLUTTERS HER EYES AT
OPHELIA. THE PRINCESS SMILES BACK.

Ophelia: What you say is true, you ugly Marcellus, you turd of men. With your help, I have cleared the way of male suitors so that my hand can be won by my dear Sandra One, part of my dear Australian kangaroo and best-est of friends! (Ophelia embraces the Kangaroo Sisters.)

THE ENTIRE CAST COMES ONSTAGE, BOWING TO GREAT
APPLAUSE AND SHOUTS FROM THE UNSEEN AUDIENCE.
CURTAIN DOWN. POLONIUS MAKES HIS WAY OUT FROM
BEHIND THE CURTAIN, ADDRESSING THE AUDIENCE.

Polonius: And so it is that our dear Hamlet died on a Fry-day that was really a Wednesday. Thank God he was scrambled and not fried. But, audience, don't you worry, our king went over-easy. He's now on the sunny side up and definitely on a better plate. And here I was, used for bait by my daughter, my scorn-filled Ophelia, as were three good men, including King Egg Hamlet. So let this be a lesson to all young hooligans. Trust not your heart, but let your mind be your judge. Women named Ophelia are not only your judge, but jury and hangman too. And as we close our play, let that be the lesson to you!

APPLAUSE. STAGE LIGHTS DOWN.
AUDIENCE HOUSE LIGHTS UP.

THE CURTAIN COLLAPSES, REVEALING ALL OF THE CHARACTERS, INCLUDING KING HAMLET, MAKING LOVE.

CAST:
Hamlet—Frank M.
Ophelia—Edith W.
Polonius—Sean of Causkeys Bar, Eyeries Village,
County Cork, father to Ophelia
Marcellus—Brendan of Bantry Psychiatric Unit, Danish soldier
Claudius—Niall, also of Bantry Psychiatric
Unit and Ophelia's would-be lover
Ciara, Sandra One, and Sandra Two—the three-
headed kangaroo (of Bantry Psychiatric Unit)
Sheila—chief royal provisioner, also of Bantry Psychiatric Unit
Guard George—George from Causkeys Bar

Editor's Note: Being one of the most important texts that define the English language and literature, *Hamlet* is a favorite among scholars. The philosophy and tragic beauty behind Hamlet make it one of the best tragedies ever written. And what are tragedies without beautiful dialogues? Unfortunately, the writers of this stage play cannot lay a similar claim. Take it or leave it, and with apologies to Bard Wil, we hope you've enjoyed our brief endeavor.

HARLEY

By William Joseph Leece

1971. New high school teacher. And I was that new teacher. Something you need to know about new teachers. They do not teach the humanities or advanced placement classes; they are given the freshman classes and the basic classes. For good reason. These classes are testing grounds, and any minor damage these new teachers might do can be corrected by the older, more experienced teachers whom students will have in the remaining three years of their high school career.

So my classes were filled with freshmen: one semester, Introduction to Literature, and second semester, with different students, Introduction to Composition.

And there I was in the springtime of my teaching years: first class in the morning, and he slumped in the back row, seat closest to the door. He had midnight black hair, Elvis Presley–style—feathered at the back carefully like a duck's ass—and velcroed to his body, a black leather jacket, collar up, and on the front a circular crest that read: HELL ON WHEELS, and his name was Harley.**Harley like motorcycle? Like motorcycle gang, perhaps? Really? And in my class.**Every morning. Early.

Not far from the school was a roller rink, Orbit, where my wife and I would roller skate on Saturday nights. Back in the '70s, these roller skates were the kind with four wheels, positioned like wheels on a car, not to be confused with the more modern rollerblades. At Orbit, you could rent two sets for a few bucks, and the rental included clean white socks. So my wife and I would circle Orbit on wobbly legs while speakers throbbed:

Singin joy to the world
All the boys and girls now
Joy to the fishes in the deep blue sea
Joy to you and me
And if I were king of the world
Tell you what I'd do
throw away the cars and the bars and the war
Make sweet love to you
Orbit was a great place for couples to spend a Saturday night.

It happened on one of those Saturday nights. The music stopped, the lights dimmed, and over the intercom system a voice announced: "Clear the rink. CLEAR THE RINK!" What happened next was absolute magic. A light flashed on the disco ball hanging over the center of the rink, and onto the rink they came. These were the practiced roller skaters, the ones who really knew their stuff. Some of them even had little battery-run lights on their skates. They twisted. They pivoted. They soared. They pirouetted—ballet on roller skates. My wife and I watched, amazed. But there was something about one of the skaters. Most were female. This one was a male. And the hair and the black jacket. Yes, yes, it was my Harley—my hell-on-wheels Harley. When the performance ended, I waited for him at the edge of the rink and shook his hand in congratulations.

Monday morning, early, he was back in my classroom: same seat, same hair, same jacket, same crest, but he smiled at me, and I smiled back.

***

This happened at the beginning of my teaching career. My job was to teach students, but there was a student, Harley, who taught me—a lesson about a black leather jacket couching a tender secret, the softness of poetry hidden in a hard shell, darkness shrouding light. I continued teaching for three more decades: same school, same classroom. Often, I thought about Harley, and always, I would smile and think a thanks.

MELANCHOLY

This happened during my second, maybe third year of teaching high school, an Introduction to Literature class for freshman students. It was probably November. November in Chicagoland is depressing. The weather can't make up its mind—should I rain or should I snow? The sky is a frequent pewter gray, and on that day, she walked into my class. I can't remember her name, but I am absolutely positive she was Irish: all that flaming red hair, the splash of freckles on her face, and she was tiny, more of the size of a fifth or sixth grader, the tiniest student at Rolling Meadows High School. I'm quite certain her parents were leprechauns. But she had a big-girl voice when she announced, "Oh, Mr. Leece, Mr. Leece, I feel so melancholy." *Melancholy.* Imagine that word coming from a tiny thirteen-year-old. And then another student added, "I feel that way sometimes, too, especially on days like this." And a third student, taking his seat in class, asked, "Mr. Leece, could we talk?" Now, I was a new teacher, but I knew that, "Could we talk?" didn't mean they wanted to talk to me. And the rules had been established early in the semester: Pull desks together in groups of three or four. No one dominates the conversation. No cross talk. Before speaking, that student must repeat something the student prior said. Those were the rules, and melancholy was in the air, so I said yes.

Quickly, quietly, they broke into small groups. Off in a corner, I sat at my desk. I don't know if they talked about being melancholy or if they talked about what it was like being in high school or the upcoming winter dance or something about parents or brothers or sisters or teachers or war or music. I don't know, but they talked for the entire period, and I didn't.

Now this was a literature class; I was well prepared, had a lesson plan introducing *Romeo and Juliet*. In my silence, I thought about the word melancholy and *Romeo and Juliet,* children of two dysfunctional families, some ancient wrong, and suicide. Melancholy? Wait until Shakespeare and I were finished with these freshmen. But I'd made a decision. *Romeo and Juliet* could wait.

***

Again, I was the teacher, but the students taught me. From them, I learned that silence is a great teacher. Teachers, certainly this teacher, talked too much. And do I follow the lesson plan in my head or follow that voice in my heart? My students taught me to follow my heart, my most important lesson about teaching. About living too.

The Never-Ending Christmas

by

Kristin Wall & Tom Richards

Dedicated to Bernadette Richards
Loving mother, grandmother, and friend
(Bernie, you always wanted me to write a Christmas story.
Well, here it is—with major help from daughter Kristin!)

About the Story:

Many years ago, back in the late 1980s, when my three children (Kristin, Cathy and Jonathan) were small, we moved to Kentstown, County Meath, Ireland. It was a rural community and a world apart from the busy market town my kids had grown up in: Navan also in County Meath. At that point, I was working me arse off trying to survive. I'd get up early to go to work and come home late. That said: I did my best to spend time with the kids despite being exhausted.

This story comes from that period of family life. On some nights, I'd walk into the kids' bedroom. There, we'd create stories. I didn't know right away what kind of story to tell, but one of my favorites was "Peter and the Wolf" and "Hansel and Gretel." I wanted something like that because I thought the kids would think it fun.

The story below started out entitled *The Never-Ending Story*. It featured a wicked witch (which lived in a dark forest and a small cabin) and a wishing well. This became sort of a game. As my daughter Kristin (now almost forty) recounts, I'd draw pictures using bright marking pens on the wall of their bedroom (which we planned to have repainted) and, based on those drawings, we'd make up the story. By the end, we'd covered all the walls in that room with various colours of markers.

In the story, the fictitious kids, the protagonists of the story, would somehow fall from Earth into this land of make-believe. They were captured by the wicked witch, and so the game began. I can't remember the details (and neither can Kristin), but she and her brother, Jonathan, and sister, Cathy, could win 'balls of magic' as prizes by answering a question. Or maybe they'd have to find the balls hidden somewhere in their bedroom. Anyway, they'd pretend to throw the balls into a magic well that had no bottom. If they won (and everyone was a winner) they'd get a point, and with enough of them, the fictitious characters in the story could escape the clutches of the ruthless witch. It was a story that had no ending, and we could have played it on and on until they were all grown up.

As Kristin says: "It wasn't the story. It was the content of the story. It is just such a brilliant memory because you made it that way, Dad. We had fun painting on the walls, and Terry (the painter) couldn't cover it because you used a marker."

(As I remember, Terry had to paint the walls ten times to cover up the story. As I say, it's a *never-ending* story, and those images are probably still there, buried under a tonne of paint, to this day.)

"You gave us your time it may have been only fifteen minutes before bed," continues Kristin, "but that was *our* fifteen minutes. Just the four of us together."

One of the biggest regrets I have to this day is that I didn't get to spend as much time as I wanted to with my kids. Many parents then and today face the same stark choice: we either work too many hours a week to make a living, or work any number of jobs, and some of us may face eviction and, perhaps, starvation. My heart goes out to those unfortunate souls, especially to single parents who are struggling all over the world. Some hold down three jobs to pay the rent, and even with local social welfare, it still may not be enough.

This is a *short*, short story. I'm going to try to write it so it can be easy to read and won't take much time. Substitute your own kids' and grandkids' names (or even your pets) for my kids' names (they're CAPITALISED in the story) as you go along. I'll also try to write it so that you can make up more story. After all, it's a never-ending story, and nothing will stop you. All you have to do is use your imagination. I'm NOT suggesting you paint on your walls, but what the hay—it was great fun! So many good wishes to all you parents and grandparents and children and grandchildren. And a Happy Christmas from Ireland—Tom & Kristin

One fine day in the land of reality, three kids named KRISTIN, CATHY, and JONATHAN waited for DAD to come home. (*Note: substitute your family's names with those in caps. And remember, you can add as many kids and adults as you want to!)* They knew he worked too hard to keep bread on the table, and their MUM thought he looked exhausted, but that's what he had to do! Yet every night, especially as Christmas grew closer, they pleaded with him to take them far away, to a Land of Nod, before it was time to go to bed.

"Sure I will!" Dad stated. "Get into yer PJs, and I'll come into your room. Then after the story, it's off to the Land of Nod and not a moment too soon!"

The kids huddled together on one single bed as Dad walked in to tell the tale, one that could be read even by them.

"Oh, Daddy," said Cathy. "Don't read to us, please. We'd rather you make one up, and don't you tease—don't start it if you're not going to finish it, or we'll take you over our knees!"

So Dad grabbed a few markers, all bright colors like Christmas. But as he began to think of a tale, all he could think of was an Easter Bunny tale (and here's what he drew).

"That tale is lousy," said Jonathan as he sucked on a Dodie (pacifier).

His pacifier was all wet, and as Dad wagged a finger, he made a new rule: "I'm only telling you a story if you get rid of that Dodie! Yer a young man now, and that Dodie is out of yer bed, or I'm done with you!"

"But, Dad, it's not Easter," Kristin complained as she looked at the drawing. "It's almost Christmas, so why not a Christmas tale full of Santa's and sleighs and a thousand tiny reindeer, including a new one named Blister!"

Dad scratched his big head which was now white and balding. "But I'm at a loss to think of a Christmas story. How about a Halloween one, with witches from the east? You realize, don't you, that Ireland started the legend of Halloween magic, the first to think of eating roast beast."

"But it's Christmas. It's Christmas!" the kids all demanded. "Now what about it, Dad? Your imagination has soured, and that's saying the least!"

So Dad thought some more and came up with a plan. "Okay, how about a never-ending Christmas story? That way, you'll never again complain that I don't read to you in bed."

The children snuggled closer as Dad got out a big pen. With markers and pens, he drew a big witch, one that swallowed kids if they didn't quite win.

"But that's upside down!" whimpered Cathy. "Can't you just do it right? Kristin was correct. We need a couple of kids and some reindeer, or a Christmas story it isn't, and you'll soon be all wet!"

So Dad drew again, and this is what he came up with:

"That's more like it," Jonathan said.

But Dad looked exhausted as he took out his pipe and lit it. "Okay, let's make a start before I fall over, or this never-ending tale will never get past a beginner. And I'll be sailing to England, and this tale will be called the 'Story of Dover'!"

And so at last, he began

> One day in the Land of Nod, there were three kids, named Kristin, Cathy, and Jonathan. All were bored, having come back from school, and all they wanted was a Christmas tale, so they decided to break the rules.
>
> They left the house quietly when Mum was making dinner
> And went to a farmhouse, and a spring well that looked even thinner
> Than the farmer's wife, and that's the full truth
> They looked over its brim, and by Santa, didn't they fall in!"

"They really fell in?" Cathy asked with wonder.

"Isn't that what I just said? Now listen to the story, or you know what? I'm off to bed." Dad cleared his throat and started again.

> Down the well they went, darker and darker, and when they came to the bottom, they hit a big steel sled. They slid on their bellies and popped into the air, with the sled flying through the air, and they realized—it was Santa's bed! Away they all went, like a down through a thistle, till they came to a dark forest, and Jonathan gave a whistle!
>
> "Look at that wood cabin, there near a tree, and isn't that a witch looking at me?"
>
> The children all looked, and what did they hear? "Come down here, you kids. I've got lunch on, and it's made of tough steer!"

"Poor cow," cried Cathy.

"Poor us," whimpered Kristin. But all Jonathan did as they thumped to the ground was to grab the witch's wand and she sang a grand song:

"Oh children, children, come here to me
This steer isn't good enough for an evil one like me.

My name is Ezmerelda, and don't you quite see?
I'll make lunch of the three of you, One, Two and Three!!!"

The RICHARDS kids began to tremble, but Jon-Jon stood up. "Vanish, you witch, Ezmerelda or not!" And he waved the magic wand, and she was tied up in knots!

"Woe is me," said the witch to the kids. "I'll tell you what. Let's play a game, and if I win, I get to eat you. But if you pull the wool over my black eyes and you win the game, why you can go home again, just as you came!"

"Game, what game?" asked Cathy. "Is it the same as hurling that we play at school? Is it that kind of game?"

"Nonsense," smirked the witch, "that game is too tame. My game is called witch ball, and here's how it's played."

She reached under her pointed hat and extracted a magic ball that glowed with witchcraft, but that's not all It spun and spat magic dust on them all!

Then she gave them each a similar ball, and they floated to the magic well, that acted like a net, for this one game of witchcraft ball at Christmas.

"Witch Ball is easy, if you know how," croaked the witch who had turned into a frog. "Just throw the ball down the well, and you get one single point. But if you miss, I get two throws and might make two points."

Kristin was the eldest, so she was up first. Down into the well, it fell, and that's not all. Up from its depths came a small reindeer named Pall Mall!

"That's one for you," cried the witch. "Now it's my turn, so get out of my way. Now I throw for Santa, and I could eat him all day!"

The witch threw, and do you know what? She got a score, and up popped Santa as big as our garage door!

"Oh, Richards kids, I'm so glad you came. This witch took me prisoner one fine spring day. If you don't win, I'm sorry to tell, there won't be a Christmas this year, because she also captured my deer!"

Cathy was next up, and she looked at Santa with a big smile. "This is easy 'cause I score all the time with my white Zlither ball." Taking careful aim, she used a big branch to strike right into the well! And when she did, up popped three reindeer looking fit as a fiddle!

It was the ugly witch's turn now, but Jonathan blocked her hit with his hurley stick, and then hit the wart on her nose which made the witch cry. He took aim and fired, and the *sliotar* (ball for playing hurling) went right into the magic well! When that happened, up popped Mrs. Claus too!

So now the Kids' Happy Christmas Team was leading. But when the witch came up for her final hurly try, the kids' grandma, GRANDMA RICHARDS, and the Clauses were captured by the witch.

Then the kids flew to the moon on a magic rainbow, and nine tiny reindeer came too to plan their attack to free everyone. There's Dasher and Prancer and Comet and Blitzen and can you name the rest?

And the lead of the team has a big ruddy red nose. Can you guess his name, too, or you'll have to touch your big toes!

When the kids get done planning, and the red-nosed reindeer blows his nose to make it glow, down to earth they all flew using Christmas dust that was the color of a single rose.

(Now, listen, kids. From here on you must whisper! Because we have to be quiet so the witch doesn't know what we plan!)

Back on Earth, they landed on the roof of their house, and the three of them flew down the chimney as quick as a mouse!

In the living room, they saw a tall Christmas tree, that Mum had named Monica, a nurse as pretty as can be!

Creeping around the tree they did sail, when Monica shouted, "Get your parents out of jail!"

"It's a talking Christmas tree," Cathy did wail. "What will we do, 'cause listen to the clock"

And the three of them strained to hear mum's grandfather clock.

It was one minute to midnight when out on the lawn, there arose such a clatter, they broke into song!

"Oh Christmas tree,
Oh Christmas tree
now tell US
WHO COULD THAT BE!"

"It's the Witch," the tree screeched, "who wants to stop Christmas If she doesn't get her way by midnight, she'll have your parents and grandma for breakfast!"

Jonathan looked around, and lo did he see a hurley stick and sliotar right under the Christmas tree!

"Look what I found," said my son with a face. "I'm gonna pound the witch to mincemeat, and we'll have a big feast, of wicked witch pancakes with mustard on top It's good for her warts and her warlock husband but not good for us!"

When the Witch came down the chimney with care, she looked around the living room, and who was right there?

Three kids: Kristin and Cathy and Jonathon too waiting near the tree with a monkey named Zoo!

So you think that's the end of the story, do you? "No way," said Zoo. "It ends RIGHT HERE!"

The author interrupts this broadcast with a special advertisement for:

Trademarked Witches Brew ™

Add one witch wart, then a warlock toe. Stir into a pot with a bunch of nettles and toss in the nearest well. Then stand welllll back, 'cause the witch will come get you tonight She's right under

your bed!!!!

Now back to our story

When Jonathan saw the witch, he picked up the stick and banged her over her head to make pumpkin bread (recipe not provided!).

vThen he knocked her on her feet and with the sliotar at the ready. He pounded her in the tummy till she was a mass of spaghetti!

That was the end of the wicked witch. She turned into smoke and disappeared up the chimney with a screech and a wail. Then she dashed her head thin upon a farmer's milking pail.

And croaking one last time, her fat butt hit an electricity pole, and it was a right electric poke! Oh, what a joke!

Now children. It's only nine-thirty by the grandfather clock. Time for bed, as the kids welcome back grandma, Tom, and Bernie too. So give Monica the Christmas tree a kiss on the cheek, and say goodbye till next time, when Rudolph won't Stink!

Oh, but wait, the kids will grow up to adults, don't you think?

And they'll have kids of their own who might read this I, the writer, does think.

So that's not the end of this story, not by half. In a few years, your children will read this and laugh. It's a never-ending story, that's what the title does spell, so don't you worry it will start all over again!

HAPPY CHRISTMAS, EVERYONE! God's blessing on you and your parents and your brothers and sister if you have some.

Remember that many don't have parents at all. They grow up in foster homes, and they do pretty well. As for siblings (what's that mean?) some of you don't have them this year. But next year, you never know, your parents could have a sister or brother. So

BE OF GOOD CHRISTMAS CHEER!

Happy Christmas to you all from Storylines Entertainment Ltd. and from our Cast of Characters. Sleep well and don't fight—and to all A GOOD CHRISTMAS NIGHT!

Cast of Characters:
Bernie and Tom—Grandparents
Grandma Richards—Mary Richards
Kristin—Kristin
Cathy—Cathy
Jonathan—Jonathan
The Tree—Monica the Nurse
And a Cast of Millions because you can all take
part in this simple story of good cheer!

THE END

(BUT IT'S NOT—IT'S ONLY A BEGINNING!)

Tommy Murray Poetry & Short Stories by Tommy Murray

(Printed with permission from Carmel Murray, his daughter)

Tommy Murray was one of the most prolific poets and short story writers in Ireland. Beloved by the residents of his hometown of Trim, County Meath, Ireland, his death left a hole in the heart of the people he loved. When he passed at the age of eighty, he left behind his wife Josie and five daughters.

Carmel Murray, the loving partner of Tom Richards, loved Tommy deeply.

A winner of many awards, this section is transcribed from his original books of short stories and poetry. We will reference those books in hopes that more can be found because Tommy, a self-publisher, paid for only a few hundred books for each publication. If you, the reader, find any of these, you may want to notify the Trim Historical Society or the Trim Writing Club.

I pay tribute to Tommy, who should have been my father-in-law, but he died too young. I wish I had known him better.
—Tom Richards

(The following are transcribed from his book of poetry, *The Boyne*, by Tommy Murray, undated.)

RIVER SCENE

And I just live for those
Mind-bending sunsets
Those shimmering dew-drenched spectacles
That linger over cellophane pools
And sparkling ripples
And mingle with
The early evening mist
Images that still remain parked
In my memory, conjuring up visions
Of silver streams
Where the latest hatch
Of midge and sedge tantalize
The denizens of the deep water
Above the chattering falls
Here, where the road ahead
Is a necklace of stepping stones
And fifteen minutes is a lifetimeThe black nymph
And blue winged olive
Take center stage

KINGFISHER

For weeks I waited
And watched, eyes patrolling the baldness
Beyond the reed beds and the rocks
Consoled only by the thought that you were
Never really a poster
That except for those rare concessions to
farmers
And fishermen between total eclipses
And the occasional catwalk you might not

even exist
And then you came
Cutting a swathe through the centuries with a
sparkling confection of
Greenish blue and orange.

(The following poems are transcribed from *Around the Rock*, a book of
literary and historical tours of Trim, County Meath, 2006)

THE ECHO GATE

My love affair with the Echo Gate
Began long before time and circumstances
Had robbed me of my innocence
Before some well-meaning friends
Had explained the mystery
Behind the voice which sounded
So uncannily like my own
"It's not a leprechaun or an ogre."
They said. "It's just your own voice
Bouncing off the abbey walls."
For me the revelation was devastating.
Yet not enough to completely destroy
My fascination with this loquacious landmark
Even to this day I could never see myself
Walking past without stopping to test the echo
At least say, "Hello."
Nor did the echo ever fail
Indeed the cross talk could go on for hours,
Yet I never seemed to get the last word, still
It's a way of life in these parts.
A custom that has outlasted
Grander and nobler devotions
A ritual rooted in childhood myths and legends.

STELLA'S COTTAGE

Stella's cottage
Smothered in autumn now
Its shrunken walls still fighting off the fields

As youngsters we used to sack potatoes there
On damp days under the tinder-dry thatch
Hunkered and cramped
As we rummaged among the gaunt growths
For Pink and Banners

And the odd Golden Wonder
Rubbing shoulders with the riff-raff
And where 'tis said
Forbidden fruit once flourished
And angels strayed in from the straight and narrow
We slung poreens through the rough door
Without as much thought for the ghost
That might have stood on the step

Stella's cottage
Struggling with September
What ghost stands there now?
My sack is full, youth
A crumpled pile in the corner
The thatch as given way to bramble, sprig and sky
And by the rough door wild potatoes pose
For puzzled passersby
So what ghost stands there now?
What spirit lurks in that skipful of briars by the roadside.

THE MONGREL
(The following short story is transcribed from *Meath Writers Anthology*)
Walk, it must be nearly two days since I heard that word. Two whole
days and still no sign of Paddy, and if that wasn't enough, two whole days

chained to the garden gate. I find this most unusual, me, the family pet, chained. Just wait till Paddy hears about this.

Walk, what wouldn't I give to hear that word again, Paddy standing at the back door, brandishing the lead, me springing forward to meet him, the fun we would have after Paddy attached the lead and ran his fingers under the collar to make sure it wasn't too tight. Then out on the high road, meeting all the neighbors, Kelly's cocker spaniel, McDonald's Labrador. Oh, do I wish Paddy would hurry up. Twice now the sun has climbed over the back garden wall, twice the shadow of the coal shed has crept halfway up the clothesline, and still no sign of Paddy.

Maybe he has gone to a football match? After all, he is the outdoor type. Football, hurling, that sort of thing, and, of course, walking beside me. Every evening after tea, as soon as he had rinsed his mug and turned it upside down upon the draining board, "Reach for the lead," he would call out across the lawn. He never had to call twice. Sometimes, he wouldn't have to call at all. From the moment that he arrived home from work I would have been watching his every move. I knew the whole routine, the old Vauxhall Viva gunning up the hill, the car door banging, the bolt being drawn, the strong smell of burned oil, pipe smoke, tea.

Lying here now on the lawn waiting for Paddy to come back, there is little for me to do except think. As a dog, I do not have an imagination and can only remember things that have actually happened. I heard Paddy reading this out of a book once. I've hardly slept a wink since the incident at the crossroads, and I have to keep one eye open just in case my master comes back. The sun is between the variegated poplar and the laburnum now, and I keep thinking about the ambulance with the flashing lights. The driver had a uniform and a peaked cap. I hate men with uniforms and peaked caps, postmen, policemen; they threaten to walk me into the ground with their big boots however much I bark.

I don't think Paddy likes policemen. He once told me that I didn't belong to him. That was the time I chased the postman away from the door. I just managed to get him before he made it to the front gate. A policeman called to the house the next day and took some particulars. He told Paddy that I was entitled to one bite. I remember Paddy's words: "He's not my dog. He strayed in here a few days ago, and I took pity on him." The postman never called after that, and Paddy would go to the post office after that for the letters.

Then there were times when Paddy was proud to be my owner. He once told some people that we met out walking that I was a creature of doubtful pedigree, which must be good because he patted me on the head at the same time. For my own part I suspect that I am a mongrel, a particularly popular breed on our street, according to Paddy.

One thing I do hate thinking about is cats, especially big black cats that sit on garden walls well out of reach and only come down into the garden at night when I am locked up. Paddy doesn't like cats either. Once he got up out of bed in the middle of the night, didn't even put on his clothes, and roared out the window at them. "Bastards," he called them and awakened the whole neighborhood. Actually, I think he prefers hedgehogs. We both like hedgehogs, especially flat ones. Once, we came across the steamrolled remains of one outside the factory gate. It had been lying there for months, gathering dust. Some boys coming home from school stopped to examine it and decided to make a frisbee out of it. They threw it, and Paddy caught it and threw it back. I kept jumping up and trying to catch it. We had such fun, and that game of Frisby went on for hours. Yes, I am certain that Paddy liked hedgehogs. He doesn't like road hogs though. He would go on and on about them, talking to himself, he would. "Bloody road hogs!" he roared at them. I myself have never seen a road hog and often wondered what they looked like. But with no imagination, that would be impossible. Much bigger than hedgehogs, I expect.

Another game we used to play was catch the sheet. When the sun was high over the telephone wires, Paddy would stretch out on the sunbed, pull a sheet over his head, and pretend to be asleep. I would pull it off again, and Paddy would chase me around the garden and let on to be vexed. Actually, that was my favorite game.

Lately, I notice Paddy has started going to football matches and leaving me at home. Ever since that time I strayed on to the pitch. How proud I was that morning, seated on Paddy's lap. The bus was full of men with blue-and-white flags. Paddy had an extra-large flag, and he was waving it out the window. I had a blue-and-white ribbon tied around my neck. "Is that your lucky mascot?" one of the men said, pointing at me. "Sure is," Paddy answered, and everyone laughed. Coming home wasn't as good. All the men were sad, and the flags were in a heap at the back of the bus. Actually, that was the only time Paddy was ever angry with me. "You're in the paper," he said to me the next day. "Do you want me to spell it out for you?" he asked, pointing to the back page. "Stray Dog Causes Lapse in United's Defense." Yes, that was when he stopped bringing me to football matches.

The sun is between the laburnum and the lilac now, and I must have dozed off because someone has brought me a meal: an extra-large plate of meaty chunks, a bowl of water, and a great big bone. This sure is unusual. I'll bet Paddy is behind it. On the other hand, he didn't believe in big meals. "There's nothing so disgusting as a big, fat, well-fed dog," he once said. It's hard to know just what is going on.

Of course, not all the things I think about are nice, and indeed, some of them can be quite disturbing. Like the evening before they chained me to the gate. We had been out walking, approaching the crossroads we were, when Paddy decided to let me off the lead. He considered me very street-wise and had no hesitation in allowing me to run free. It was nearing sundown, and the big bullocks were just beginning to elbow their way through the sheep on Canty's hill. The verges were full of new and exciting scents. Paddy seemed to be in a thoughtful mood, and indeed, I would have been, too, if I had an imagination. He was probably thinking of our garden back home basking in the half light, the midges dancing over the gooseberry bushes and the pot marigolds folding up for the night. I, on the other hand, was completely taken up with a movement in the shrubs on the other side of the road. A cat, I figured, well worth investigating. Probably one of the creatures that so annoyed Paddy that night. "Wouldn't he be proud of me if I chased it away once and for all?" Here goes, l thought to me, and dashed across the thoroughfare.

The next thing I remember was a car swerving. A screech of brakes and a loud bang followed. Next thing I saw was Paddy lying on the side of the road, groaning. Then a crowd gathered, and people were standing around nodding. Someone mentioned a road hog, and another pointed at me. A policeman was measuring the road and writing in a little book. Then they were putting Paddy on a stretcher and carrying him toward the ambulance. Someone pulled a sheet over Paddy's face, which I thought a bit silly because the sun wasn't shining. I, of course, wasn't having any of this. Indeed, I felt obliged to pull the sheet off again. It was then that the policeman came rushing at me with a heavy stick. I must have blacked out, but not before I managed to bite him on the wrist. "You've had it, boy," he said, and the next thing I found myself here, chained to this gate.

The sun is between the lilac and the smallest of the gooseberry bushes now, and I can hear voices coming. There is a policeman standing at the gable end of the house. A man with a shop coat and Wellington boots is approaching the garden gate. He has some sort of needle or syringe in his hand, and he is smiling. He really does seem nice. I expect that he is going to take me to see Paddy.

No Place Like Home

By Tom Richards
A tragi-comedy & postscript to the novel
Always Come Home by Tom Richards,
written as an involuntary patient in
Bantry Psychiatric Unit, late March 2022.
With always, my loving partner in mind as I write, Carmel Murray.

Dedicated to best friend
Frank McQuaid,
the nurses, doctors, and staff of Bantry
Psychiatric Unit & Carmel Murray

A SPECIAL NOTE TO DOCTOR MUSHTAQ:
My dear doctor: please understand that every novel, screenplay,
and stage play requires a villain to create dramatic tension. Note
that this time, it is you! Thank you for everything, especially your
professional concern. Signed, Tom Richards, your patient.

For over twenty years, David Bloom spent time in the Bantry Psychiatric Unit under the care of various clinical psychiatrists, nurses, and staff, and in the company of an ever-changing litany of those visited by the dark shadow of mental health difficulties. Every four to six months, David would again be visited by what his psychiatrists called "the dark shadow of insanity." Upon those visits, David would again descend into complete psychosis. At those times, he would be locked, alone, into seclusion: a twenty-foot by fifteen foot dungeon which did more to make him insane than even his crazy head psychiatrist.

His medical team was astonished by the variety of unmoving poses he would take. His rigid body could stand for hours on one foot (usually the right) with his arm extended toward the ceiling, his finger pointing toward the single square of reinforced glass. Or he would squat, his buttocks only an inch off the floor. At other times, he might sit for hours on the cold linoleum tiling, his head rotated uncomfortably to the left, his chin on his shoulder.

During these times of stillness, David Bloom never made a sound.

Rachel, his adult daughter, made it a point to fly over from Long Island, New York, twice a year, usually in midsummer and then just after Christmas. During those trips, she always had discussions with her father's latest psychiatrist on what might make David better. She lost count of her trips at twenty-two journeys. As the years went on, her father's hair began to fall out, her own starting to show graying streaks. Each time she checked into the Bantry Hotel near the psychiatric unit, Rachel wondered what new cocktail of medication her keepers had prescribed to the man she used to call Dad and adore. She still adored him, but the man she had known all her life wasn't there anymore.

Something of a breakthrough occurred eighteen years following David's first detention in the psychiatric unit. A new drug had been developed with a strange-sounding name she could not get her tongue around: psycho-nestorin. As Rachel entered the single bedroom where her father now slept, she noted that his present psychiatrist, Dr. Jamal, hovered anxiously over him with a hand on her father's forehead. The doctor held a penlight, washing her father's closed eyes with the bright beam of light.

"Mr. Bloom?" he asked softly, and Rachel stepped quickly toward the bed. Jamal looked up at her, his broad smile filling her field of vision.

"Is he okay?"

"I think," the doctor said in his sing-song Pakistani accent, "that he is at last coming back to us."

Rachel leaned close to her father, pulling back her long hair that had been disheveled by her long plane ride. "Dad, it's Rachel. Open your eyes, Dad. Look at me."

Her father's eyelids fluttered slightly. Finally, the left eye opened fully though the right one remained closed. She watched as his right hand moved swiftly, like a snake striking. His sweating fingers took her wrist in a vice-like grip.

"Dolores?" he croaked. Then he closed both eyes and passed out.

Rachel called her husband, Jacob, using her cell phone, in the small waiting area, briefing him on this glorious turn of events. "He said something, Jacob. Dad hasn't uttered a word in years."

Standing in the large office of his New York law practice, Jacob paced the thick carpeting and then stopped, gazing sightlessly out the large window at a glittering Hudson River. "He talked? Rachel, what did he say?"

"He said her name, Jacob," she uttered sadly. "He called for Dolores."

"And not for you," he replied. As they hung up, Jacob realized that single word of lost love had once again broken his wife's heart.

"That's what you said, David," Jamal stated pointedly. "You called her name."

Dressed only in a robe and pajamas, David shook his head. "I don't remember. I don't remember anything."

The doctor paused. His patient couldn't remember anything in over twenty years? Dr. Jamal had never read about a fugue state lasting that long. His observations could prove critical to future psychiatric care.

"You don't know who Dolores is?" Jamal asked carefully. "Think back to when you were a boy. Doesn't her name mean anything to you?" David Bloom shook his head. "Then perhaps you could tell me how you feel?"

It took a minute for his patient to find the words. "Weak. Hungry."

The doctor's thin face broke into a smile. "Those issues can be taken care of immediately! Nurse!" he called, then bent over and grasped his patient by the arm. "Rachel is here. She would like to have dinner with you."

"Rachel?"

"Do you remember who Rachel is, David?"

David's lips broke into a warm smile. "My daughter."

They ate together in a small antechamber just off the unit's dining room. As she ate, Rachel studied her father's face. He wore a shirt, jumper, and jeans, all of which were too large because he'd lost so much weight. She made a mental note to run up to Cork City for a new wardrobe for him. She watched as her father shoveled one forkful of roast beef and mashed potato after another into his mouth. In minutes, he had cleaned his plate.

"Do you want some more?"

He shook his head, pushing away his tray. "Not now. Maybe later."

Rachel reached out, taking her father's hand. "Dad, Dr. Jamal says that you don't remember who Dolores is."

David thought a moment and shook his head. "I don't remember the name at all."

Rachel smiled. "Maybe it's for the best."

David pushed his chair back. "What's next? Any idea?"

"I talked to the doctor before we ate. He wants you to stay here for another week. But then he made a promise to both of us."

Bloom frowned. "Which is?"

"If we can get you fit, he wants you to go home. It's time."

David Bloom felt an involuntary shudder crawl up his spine. "You're sure? That's what he said?"

When she nodded, Bloom felt the weight of the world lift from his shoulders. For years back at his American home of Long Island, New York, he'd yearned for two things, both promises that he had made to himself. The first was to go back to Ireland and visit his parents' home to confront the ghosts of his past. As for the second he couldn't remember it at all. All he knew was that it had nothing to do with a woman named Dolores.

Two days later, David found himself sitting in the passenger seat of Rachel's rental car. His window was wide-open, and as he looked out on Bantry Bay, which glittered silver in the strong morning light, he pivoted his head and glanced up at the Miskish Mountains. They towered above him like a rocky spine, and he breathed in deeply, smelling the salt air, and felt a sense of freedom. Twenty minutes later he caught sight of Bere Island rising tall from the choppy waters of Bantry Bay and realized that soon, he would be home. Yet in many ways he did not want to go there. The island held too many alarming memories for him: of his mother and how she had committed suicide, with her blood all over the bathroom tile floor. Hector, his father, and his anger, thinking that a young Davy had betrayed him by letting Rose die, and his father's face when he had ordered his only son to leave the house and never darken the door again.

As he thought about his home on Bere Island, he suddenly remembered Dolores and what she had meant to him. His body trembled as he realized that was the other promise he had made to himself: to find Dolores and tell her exactly how much he missed her. He wanted to say that his proposal of marriage, which he had made when he was only seventeen, was still in his heart, his love for her exactly the same as it was when he had left her fifty years earlier and fled to New York City.

He caught Rachel glancing at him, and as they rounded a bend and descended into Castletownbere, she gently placed a hand on her father's forearm.

"Dad, while you were ill, I saw a lawyer. She saw to it that I'm not only your next of kin but also your POA—power of attorney. This means that I'm the only person who has the legal right to look after you while you recover. I went to Grandpa's farmhouse when you became really ill."

"You went to Hector and Rose's house?" David asked. She nodded.

"I went the night you first became comatose. I saw everything."

"What did you see?"

She pulled over, stopping the car and turning off the engine. She couldn't look him in the eye, but instead gazed out at the cloudless sky as she remembered.

"I saw the farmhouse as it looked years ago. The house seemed new, and I could smell fresh paint. Even the grandfather clock on the staircase was ticking. I knew it was impossible because the house had long been abandoned, and you'd told me it was mostly a wreck. Then I went outside and" She stopped, not knowing what to say.

"And what?" David asked.

"I saw you and Dolores together. You were both so happy. You were both younger. You had a full head of hair, curling brown to your shoulders. You looked to be in your late teens. Dolores looked even younger. You looked so much in love. Don't you remember Dolores at all?"

David wouldn't take his eyes off Bere Island, which still rose in the near distance. "Yes, I remember the name. But Rachel, the bastards at the psychiatric tribunal told me she's dead. She died years ago." He looked over at her. "I only remembered Dolores as we came down here, and I saw Bere Island. That's where we met." He turned to her in his seat. "Let's just forget about it, okay? What you experienced was probably only a bad dream. Some sort of wishful thinking."

"But, Dad, you were happy. Happier than I've ever seen you," she replied, taking his hand. "I don't care if it was a dream or not. Maybe it was a message from her, asking me to remind you how very happy you both were together."

"Forget her," David stated, squeezing her hand in return. "What is she. A ghost? She's dead, Rachel. Gone forever. Besides, aren't I happy now, being here with you?"

As they drove on, Rachel decided not to utter another word about Dolores.

When they arrived in Castletownbere, David was surprised that Rachel didn't turn left toward the ferry that would take them to Bere Island. Instead, she turned right at the SuperValu grocery store. Accelerating, she climbed the narrow street that locals called the High Road.

"Why are we going this way?" David asked.

"It's a surprise," Rachel replied, smiling.

As the road widened, at the very top of the hill, a breathtaking panorama of life swept into view. A large, flat valley of peat and green fields was spread out before them. Yellow gorse bloomed in the bright summer sun. Three colts galloped past them on the right-hand side of the road, their bright manes billowing in the wind. One tried to leap the wire fence that kept them from running into the sparse rural traffic. To the left, at the distant horizon, David could see the broad, blue Atlantic Ocean. Rising from the sea, Scariff Island's rocky image looked like a jumping whale.

I really am free, David thought to himself. Thank God, I'm free at last.

Driving on, the car again climbed the winding road and up a steep hill. At a large brown tourist sign painted with white letters with the name of the village, Rachel made a left and descended into Eyeries. They drove past the local café and then O'Shea's Pub. David hadn't been there in years and had forgotten the village's single main street and the small two-story cottages that were painted in a rainbow of colors. Again, they ascended a hill, past Causkeys Bar and Saint Kentigern Catholic Church. He remembered how once, when he was small, he had gone with his parents to a baptism there. When the ceremony had finished, they and the other congregants had trooped across the street. David had sat on his father's lap as his parents gossiped with the local people and his mother drank a gin and tonic. Of course, this was before Rose had started drinking hard. It was a happy memory, but David closed his eyes anyway, remembering her suicide that had happened a few years later.

Rachel started to slow the car and began to pull over.

"Are we stopping?" he asked. "Why here?"

"This is your surprise," she said. Her eyes looked away from him, and he knew she was worried about his reaction. "Dad, when you were in hospital, I sold Hector and Rose's house. The proceeds were enough to buy this one for cash, with a whole lot left over." She looked across the street to a brightly painted, two-story cottage.

"You bought this for me?"

When she nodded, his gaze settled on the robin-egg-blue house, painted the same color his mother had selected, years ago, for the old family farmhouse. They both got out of the car. As they approached the front door, Rachel reached into her bag and withdrew a small silver chain with two objects dangling from it.

"Welcome to your new home," she said. "I hope you'll find happiness here."

When David took the chain, he saw a silver key which he assumed was for the front door. But swinging next to it was a gold Claddagh ring he immediately recognized.

"That can't be our old ring." He looked up at his daughter, catching her eye. "Is it?"

"I found it in the farmhouse, the same night that I saw the vision of you and Dolores. I know it's yours, and I wanted to return it to you."

Carefully, David unclipped the chain. He grasped the golden ring and turned it over. Inscribed inside, he read the tiny lettering he had not seen in so many years: *D+D forever.*

Tears formed in his eyes as he remembered his past love, Dolores. He slipped it onto a finger and, using the key, opened the front door. Slowly, he walked in, taking in the large open-plan living area and kitchen. Straight ahead, a set of stairs led up to the second floor. Rachel led the way upstairs.

"See?" she said at the top. "You've a large bedroom here to the left which you could use as the Master. A big bathroom over there and another bed in here," she said, first pointing down the hall to the bathroom, then leading him into another small, sunny room and motioning toward a second stairway. "Up there is a large attic you could use as an office." David turned around and walked into the larger bedroom. "It comes with all the furnishings?" David asked his daughter, seeing a large bed and wooden dressers for his clothes.

"Yes," Rachel answered, her eyes sparkling. "Dad, you lost everything when you're old home burned down. This house is completely furnished. All you have to do is live a new life of happiness here."

David glanced down at his hand, looking into his open palm. The ring with its large heart and Celtic shape, the one Rachel had returned, glittered in the sunlight. He knew that with their ring in his hand, Dolores was with him wherever he might go. He grinned.

"You're right. It's time to start a new life."

They exited, walking back down the stairs, hand in hand.

David settled quickly into his new life in the blue house he called Solas Mor—the Place of the Sun. He met Frank, an old Irish acquaintance and boyhood friend, at the post office soon after he moved in. They shared much in common, like a divorce and losing a business. When they first talked about their mutual challenges, David couldn't help but think of his old pal Ledbetter and wondered how he was coping in jail, where he would spend the rest of his life for fraud and racketeering. He realized that in some ways his old business partner had actually done him a favor. Through his threats and actions, Ledbetter had actually driven David back to Ireland, his boyhood home. Thanks to that bully, David was on his way to finding that new life Rachel and he had discussed.

It got to be a habit for David to walk up to Causkeys Bar most nights, only six houses up the single main road of Eyeries, where he'd have one or two pints with his new friends and laugh and stir the shite. Frank invited him to join the Four O'Clock Club with two other guys, Michael and Kieran, and informal group whose only passion was drinking a few and a lot of laughter. When he ran out of things to say or laugh about, David walked back to his house. There, he'd make dinner for one, then watch television until he went to bed alone. Always alone. It tore him up because he still missed Dolores so much.

Just once, remembering how, when he was in the Psychiatric Unit, he had come to believe Dolores was truly alive, he tried to track her down to prove her existence one way or another. He talked to the postmistress in Eyeries, who said she'd never heard of Dolores. He tried again at the post office in Castletownbere, then the one in Ardgroom. None of the people he had talked to had ever heard of her, either.

Summer was turning to autumn, and his loneliness grew larger. Then on one fine afternoon, as he stood in his shed smoking a cigarette and drinking a tin of Guinness, he looked out the shed window. Dolores was sitting at the large round outdoor table drinking a glass of Prosecco in the sun. David stumbled from the shed, walking slowly toward her.

"Dolores?" he croaked, stunned. He worried he was again experiencing psychosis and wondered if he should phone Dr. Jamal. Quickly, he took his mobile phone from his coat pocket.

"David, stop it," she giggled. "Yes, it's me."

"It can't be. They told me you're dead. And when I tried to find you, no one remembered you."

"Come over here, you eejit. Take my hand if you don't believe me."

He walked closer, almost falling over from the shock. But when he took her hand in his own, it was as solid as the wooden decking upon which he trod. Too, her hand was warm. And when he took her wrist and pressed his fingers to the back of it, he could feel the strong beating of a loving pulse.

"What are you doing here?" he whispered.

"You called for me in your dreams. Don't you remember?"

David thought back. Since moving into Solas Mor, he couldn't remember dreaming about anything. "No, I don't remember."

She laughed harder this time. "Well, I do, you fool. I was lying right next to you, just so you know. And you *did* have dreams, but they were more like nightmares. They were all about me. You looked and looked and you could never find me. Every night you'd sit bolt upright in bed, screaming my name."

"I did?" When she nodded, he could only smile back ruefully. "So now what do we do?"

"We do what we've always wanted to do. We get married and live our lives in peace and quiet."

With that, the back garden door opened. Frank walked onto the deck with an eight-pack of Guinness. He walked right past Dolores without seeing her at all. "Hey, buddy. It's almost four," Frank said to David. "How about a tin of Guinness here then we'll walk up to Causkeys?"

David was astonished and sat down on one of the table's four chairs. "Frank, can I ask you something? Do you see anyone else sitting at this table?"

Frank only grinned. "Are you kidding? Stirring the shite again, are you, Dave? So how about that beer?"

Dave thought about it for a moment as, from across the table, Dolores mouthed the words, "Go on. I'll be fine." But Dave only shook his head. "Frank, I've got a roast in the oven. Let me check on it, and I'll meet you up at Causkeys in ten minutes."

"No problem, kid. I'll see you there. Put these in the shed, and we can have them later."

Frank set the eight-pack down on the table and then left by the way he had come in.

Dave's eyes settled on Dolores. "Frank couldn't see you. What are you, Dolores? You can't be a ghost. There's no such thing."

"Aren't there? It's you who say I'm a ghost, not me," she replied, smiling. "Come on. I'll have another glass of Prosecco while you have a Guinness. There's an open bottle in the fridge."

"No there's not."

"Isn't there?" she laughed, her eyes bright in the sunlight.

When he found the open bottle—not understanding where it had come from because he rarely drank Prosecco— he brought back the drinks. Now over his initial shock, the couple toasted each other and to a new life together.

One week later, they married in the back garden. They had no need for a priest, a vicar, or even a public registrar. Their love had always been such that they didn't need to get legally wed to be married. Instead, they said simple vows they had written together.

David and Dolores stood on the back garden grass. His girl was dressed all in white with a wedding gown David had bought her in the town of Kenmare, County Cork. Her veil was a train of gossamer white; her hair was tied up loosely with strands of her auburn hair brushing both cheeks. In her hands was a large bouquet of yellow and orange roses tied together with some fuchsia, which she told him were her mother's favorite flowers. As for Dave: he wore his best dark suit and clutched the box holding their wedding rings. Both stood on the grass in bare feet.

At noon exactly, Dave looked to his bride. "Are you ready, Dolores?"

When she nodded, he opened the Bible that was his mother's, one of the few family possessions the firefighters had rescued from his parents' farmhouse fire.

"I, David Bloom, in faith, honesty, and love, take you, Dolores, to be my wedded wife. To share with you God's plan for our lives together united in Christ." When he finished, Dolores repeated the same prayer.

Then they intoned together, "David and Dolores, forever and ever. So it will be in the name of God the Almighty. In the name of the Father and the Son and the Holy Ghost. Amen."

David had bought two simple rings of gold in Kenmare. After they exchanged rings, the happy couple kissed deeply. This time, there was no inscription on the rings. A ring did not have to remind them of their mutual love. Now, rather than forever, their love would be forevermore—an everlasting eternity together.

When they finished, Dave carried his wife up to bed. There, they would express their vows in a way that any happily married couple would.

***

Frank was the only person in Eyeries to actually see her. Each morning, Frank had to deliver newspapers across the Beara Peninsula. One day, leaving at 5:30 a.m. as he usually did, he drove past his friend's blue-painted house and noticed something different. Dave's front door was ajar. He stopped and put on his van's emergency flashers.

"Hello?" Frank said, standing at the front door. "Hey, Dave? It's Frank. Your door is open."

When no one replied, he stepped in. "Hello!" he called again. "Dave?"

At the top of the stairs, a hand reached out from the bedroom to turn on the hall light. It was then that he saw her. She wore a white nightgown, her auburn hair streaming like gold over both shoulders. Her cherub face and hazel eyes glittered in the light. Frank stepped back, embarrassed, because he could see right through the thin fabric of her gown, her nipples raised, her face on fire, and he sensed that he had interrupted early morning lovemaking.

"I'm really sorry," said Frank. "I was looking for David."

He could see her blush in the light. "I'm Dolores, David's wife. Let me wake him."

When Dave came down the stairs in his gray robe, he took Frank aside. "Frank, did you really see Dolores? She told me you wanted me. I can't believe it."

"What do you mean, can I see her? Of course, I can see her. How did you find her?"

"It's hard to explain, Frank," David stated, awe-struck. "Call it a miracle romance. We were married yesterday."

"Yesterday? Why didn't you tell me you two were getting married?"

"We decided to do it on the spur of the moment. I'm sorry, Frank. If I'd had more time, I would have asked you to be my best man." Then Dave thought again. "Frank, do me a favor. Let's keep Dolores a secret between us. The other villagers may be startled by her sudden appearance. You know how some people are," and he mentioned a woman who could never mind her own business. The last thing Dave needed was word to get out to Dr. Jamal or to Rachel that he was seeing Dolores.

Frank nodded and grinned. "What, you want to keep that beauty all to yourself, huh? Okay, no problem." And they shook hands on the deal. "But you're buying me a few pints tonight, Dave. Got it?"

David grinned back. "Got it in one."

When Frank left, he went back to the bedroom. There, he found Dolores sleeping. As she snored softly, he worried that he really was insane. She can't be real, he thought to himself. This is all a moment of psychosis. I'll wake in a minute and she'll be gone. The only thing that steadied him was the knowledge that Frank had seen her, too.

He turned, walking down the hall to the bathroom, and started brushing his teeth. As he picked up his toothbrush, he noticed another one resting beside it. Feeling the bristles, he found they were wet. "Ghosts don't brush their teeth," he muttered to himself. Then he looked in the mirror. His face, lined with worry and the consequences of treatment, stared back at him. He looked not only sixty-six, but felt much older than that. Then he thought of Dolores and realized: she looked no older than the day she had first come to visit him in the Bantry Psychiatric Unit, twenty years ago. At the time, she had looked twenty-eight, as beautiful as the moment she had dropped that book on the Beara Island dock, when Prince, his black Labrador, had bounded over and Dave had asked Dolores, the two then only teenagers, to read it with him.

At that moment, standing in the bathroom, he confirmed one single fact: Dolores wasn't a ghost. She was as real and as alive as he was. She'd come back from the dead to be with him and make him the happiest man alive. 'What a wedding gift,' he thought to himself. Then he walked back to the bedroom and woke her. All that day, they did nothing but make love.

For the next eleven months, they lived a life of happiness. Soon, they talked like a couple who had been married for thirty years or more. It was as if they lived in each other's heads and learned to think each other's thoughts.

"Dave, I was thinking," Dolores might say.

"Dolores, so was I," he might reply.

"It's raining outside, but it still might be nice"

"... if we bundled up and took a walk on the beach."

By unspoken consent, they only ventured out of the house together when the village streets were empty, or if it was pitch black. Only stray dogs or sheep grazing upon the craggy coastline fields witnessed them as Dave helped his new wife climb over the larger rocks near the sea. Of course, Frank might see them if they strolled along the main street in the early morning, as he left to do his newspaper delivery round. Other than Frank, no one met Dolores. Never did she go with David to Causkeys Bar. Not once as a couple did they eat together in Castletownbere's many fine restaurants.

During their time together, Dave worried for her only once. As she carried a glass of Prosecco into the large back room with its stunning views of Coulagh Bay, she stumbled, falling flat on her face, hurting herself. He had to pick her up and wipe her nose of the blood he found there.

"Are you all right, sweetie?"

"It's nothing," she insisted. "I've just had one too many glasses of wine."

"You only had 2 glasses. I've never seen you fall like that before. You hit the floor hard. Don't you feel the blood on your face?" He wiped her apple cheek with a tissue, holding it out so she could see the blood.

"You're over-reacting. I'm fine. Honestly."

He decided to agree, but from that point on, he kept a close eye on his wife.

David learned to play golf and bought a piano. He found a song that he felt was their song, called "Long-Lost Lovers." He transcribed it together with the words, and at night before they went to bed, he played it for her as if it was their evening prayer. He started working again, this time as a member of the Cork County Council. He pushed a broom in the streets and was content to be out of Big Business. He even went back to Bere Island and asked the new owner if there was anything left of his mother's grandfather clock. When he was led to the barn, Dave found it half destroyed. But with a handshake, the owner allowed him to take it home. Together, they loaded it onto a used pickup truck Dave had bought, and he spent months working in his shed to get the grandfather clock back in working order. When he had fixed it, he and Frank carried it up the stairs of the new home and stood it at the top where Dolores and Dave could hear it tick at night as if it was his mother's beating heart.

Eventually, David grew impatient that Dolores wouldn't come out with him. "Dolores, are you ashamed of me?" Dave asked one morning. "Do you not want to be seen in public with David Bloom because he's supposed to be nuts?"

"I don't want us to be found out," Dolores replied, and he could hear fear in her voice. "I don't want anything bad to happen to you."

"Like what? No one can see you but me and Frank. Dolores, don't be a fool."

"If they see you talking into thin air, if you forget what I am, don't you see you could be taken back to the Psychiatric Unit?"

All Dave could do was laugh. Hurt, she turned on her heel, heading up to their bedroom. He waited five minutes and then called for her. "Dolores, I'm sorry." When she didn't respond, he charged up the stairs and found her packing a bag. "Where the hell do you think you're going?"

"We're finished. Done. I won't be party to something that will hurt you."

"Hurt me?" he replied, taking her into his arms. "Dolores, don't you see? If you're not real, I'm better off dead. Don't you know how much I love you?"

She returned the hug and early that night, they went to bed. Having made love, she turned to him, but he was already asleep. Little did he know that it was the last time they would make love on Earth.

"David," she whispered, not wanting to wake him, "I'll love you always, no matter what happens. But don't you see? They'll hurt you again because of me." Then she turned over and nestled against him, her legs moving under him like they were a pair of loving spoons. Then she stroked his head and took his hand in her own. In his sleep, Dave sighed with contentment. His other hand took hers, and then, for the last time, she whispered into his ear.

"Goodbye, my beautiful man. I love you. Remember, I'll always be here for you."

When he woke the next morning, Dave found that Dolores was gone. He ran into the streets, calling her name. It had begun to drizzle, and his pajamas soon became soaked. His calls echoed all over the village, waking his neighbors because it was only five-thirty in the morning. When Frank drove by, he found his friend in the middle of the road, screaming like a madman.

"What's wrong?" Frank asked Dave, stopping his van.

"Dolores is missing!"

Frank reached across, pushing open the passenger door. He gunned the engine, and they took off to Castletownbere to report Dolores missing to the local Gardaí. On the way, David realized that the drive was useless. Other than him, Frank was the only other person who could see Dolores. If Frank asked the Garda to search for her, they'd come up empty-handed.

"Frank, turn around," Dave said, squirming in his seat. "She might have gone back to the house."

"No way, buddy boy. The Garda will find her. You wait."

When they found no one at the station, Frank decided that they should go to Bantry and the large Garda station there. When they arrived, Frank insisted that they report Dolores as a missing person, and Dave sucked in a deep breath when the Garda on duty wasn't certain exactly what to do.

"She's only been gone a few hours, hasn't she?" he asked, addressing David. "Maybe you two had a fight and she stormed out."

"We never fight," David answered, deciding to go along with it.

"Dead right," Frank stated. "I've never seen a couple who's happier together."

The Garda took down Dolores's details but couldn't promise anything. "We'll try our best, but it's unlikely we'll find her. Have you tried her relatives?"

"Her parents are dead!" Dave shouted. "As far as I know, Dolores has no relatives or close friends. I don't know where she is. I'm worried for her, don't you understand that? She could be lost in the rain for all I know. Frank, didn't you notice how she could fall and hurt herself?"

Frank shook his head, glancing up at his friend. "Hey, buddy. Lower your voice. And no, I never saw Dolores fall."

Dave slammed his fist on the Station front counter. "I demand that you do something to find her right now!"

"Hey, calm down, Mister Bloom," the Garda said. "I told you we'd try to find her." The Garda signed the report, and together, Frank and Dave walked out into the rain to continue their search. As the front door swung shut, the Garda's eyes narrowed. He'd heard about Bloom and his years in the Bantry Psychiatric Unit. Rubbing his jaw, his eyes swung to the phone. Hesitating, he finally picked it up and made a call he didn't want to make.

"Could I speak to Dr. Jamal?"

Over the next two days, David's search for Dolores became more frantic. He combed the entire Beara Peninsula looking for her. From Bantry to Allihies and right up to Kenmare, he screamed and shouted her name. Those he met that he did not know considered him a madman and a menace.

As for Frank, he chose to keep his distance from his best friend. Dave's behavior had become even too much for Frank. One day, at 4:00 p.m., Frank called into Causkeys Bar for a pint. The only person in the pub was Jay, the owner. As she served him his Guinness, she noticed that Frank looked down, his head drooped toward the solid mahogany bar.

"Frank, are you all right?" she asked, perplexed because Frank was always in good form.

"No, I'm not," he said, sipping his drink. "It's Dave. His wife is missing."

"His wife? What wife? I didn't know Dave had married."

"He married Dolores."

"Dolores who?"

"Dolores Foley," replied Frank.

The owner's face screwed into puzzlement. "Does she have long auburn hair and hazel eyes?" Frank nodded. "Frank, the only Dolores

Foley I know that fits that description lived for a long time on Bere Island. She died in 1997."

"That can't be right," Frank said, putting down his pint. "I've seen her, for Chrissakes. A good-looking woman, right? She had parents that emigrated years ago, and Dolores stayed with her aunt on the Island."

The barkeep laughed. "Yes, Frank, that's right. Now why not pull the other one. The poor gersha died of cancer in Urhan. I remember hearing rumors that she and Dave were doing a number when they were in their teens." The barkeep's eyes went wide. "You don't think that poor David is having spells again, do you?"

The front door burst open, and Dave ran in. He looked frantically around the bar.

"Hey, buddy," Frank greeted him. "Why don't you pull up a stool and I'll buy ye a pint?"

But Dave was so frantic that he didn't hear his best friend. Instead, he ran back out onto the street. They could hear him screaming for his wife. "Don't you worry. I'll calm him down." Frank said to Jay. Then draining his pint glass, he walked out the door.

As soon as Frank left, the pub's phone began to ring. When Jay answered it, she found herself talking to a psychiatrist in Bantry. "Why, yes, Dr. Jamal. Dave just left. His behavior? Why, he was rather crazy. He kept calling for Dolores Foley, but Dolores passed away years ago."

As she listened further to the doctor, her eyes went wide. At that point, Frank marched back in the door. When Jay rang off, she looked Frank dead in the eyes. "That was Dave's psychiatrist. He wants you to find David and keep him distracted or maybe have him take a nap."

"Why?" Frank asked.

"Dr. Jamal fully believes that Dave is again suffering from psychosis. He's sending some men to take him back to Bantry Psychiatric Unit."

Frank nodded and walked uncertainly back out the door. The last thing he wanted was to place his friend into treatment again. He knew David could not stand even one more day of Seclusion. But because that's what the doctor ordered, Frank would follow the instructions to the letter. Dave would be better off under the psychiatrist's care. And besides, Dolores—if there really was a Dolores—would want it. Yet, hadn't he seen her? Was it a case of mistaken identity? Perhaps another Dolores

Foley had died. Whatever had happened, his best friend's behavior had become crazy. It was best to follow the psychiatrist's orders. Frank was determined to protect David from himself, and worried that he was so out of control, he might attempt suicide.

Frank finally found David in his house and insisted that he take a nap.

"Come on over here and I'll cover you up," Frank said, plumping the pillows on the couch in the back room. "Dolores wouldn't want you to get sick, would she?"

But Dave was pacing the floor. "She has to be somewhere, doesn't she, Frank? A person doesn't just disappear into thin air."

"Maybe she's gone overseas. To England, maybe, or the States."

"She scared of flying. She wouldn't go without telling me."

"Come on. Lie down for a bit. When you get some rest, we'll look again. In the meantime, I'm going to make a few more calls to see if I can track her down," he said as he let himself out the front door.

When Frank left, David lay down on the couch, covering himself with a light blanket. Just as he was falling asleep, he heard someone knocking hard on the front door. Grumbling, he got up and headed into the living room. Opening the door, he found a tall man standing at the door with two other beefy guys behind him. A blue van was parked in front of his house, blocking traffic.

"Hey, Dave, I'm Danny," the fellow said. "I just wanted to have a word with you."

Then Danny pushed hard at the front door, as if trying to break in. Dave reacted as anyone would. He tried to slam shut the door, but Danny was stronger. Dave pushed harder, his feet slipping on the kitchen tiling. Danny burst in, grabbing Dave by both wrists. David looked up. Two other men marched in, and he could see two Garda behind them. One of the goons grabbed him by the waist, and the other ran behind to block any possible escape. As David struggled, they dragged him out of the house. They pushed him into the van, a goon on each side of him as he sat in the passenger seat. The other goon climbed into the driver's seat. As the driver engaged the transmission, Dave put his head in his hands. Gazing through his fingers, he looked at a long tear scissored into the seat in front of him. The torn leather flapped as the van bounced up the main street, then onto the High Road leading to Castletownbere and Bantry. As the van drove on, David realized that he was being placed into involuntary admission to a psychiatric unit for the second time in his life.

At the Bantry Psychiatric Unit, the three Psychiatric Assisted Admission staff who had brought him to the unit throttled David, dragging him into the building. Dave started to scream: "Dolores! Rachel. Help me. Dolores!"

They stopped and to calm him, handed David a single cigarette. He dragged on it almost impulsively, as if the smoke that wafted above him could form a ladder for his escape. When he finished, he begged for a second smoke, but they denied him the pleasure. Instead, they marched him into the unit, a staff member at each side.

Inside, they forced two antipsychotic tablets down his throat. Dave gagged because he refused to take water. A male nurse grabbed him. The strong ox of a man threw him into a Seclusion room. As the door banged shut and Dave heard the lock turn tight, he screamed again but knew that no one could hear him except for the female nurse who spied on him from the monitor she looked at in the staff room. David gazed up. A video camera looked down on him like an eye in the sky. He paced to the left. The camera followed him. He paced to the right. It still followed him. In the room was only a single chair which also acted as a toilet. He broke it. Using the steel leg of the chair, he smashed the camera, then fell to his knees, sobbing. He was certain, then. The nightmare had started once again. He was asleep by eight o'clock, curled up on the cold tile floor with the benefit of only a single thin blanket.

The next morning, David was taken from Seclusion to a small room which also acted as an anteroom. On one side was an elevator door. On another a panoramic window giving views of Bantry Bay. Far off to the west, he feared that Dolores hid in the rocks. As he watched, a curtain of rain came in from the east. The wind got up, a gale for sure. Dave became anxious that his girl might perish in the coming storm.

"We hate to break in on your simple reverie," a voice called. Dave turned to find Dr. Muskrat, a man of thin frame, a mustache and beard, wearing a suit that made him look like a preacher. "I have but fifteen minutes," he said in his clipped French accent. "I understand that you are seeing things again, are you not, David?"

"Who the hell are you?"

"I am the acting head of Psychiatry at the unit. Now what do you say, Bloom? Are you seeing things or not?"

"Don't call me Bloom!" David roared. "Not even Mr. Bloom, you asshole."

Muskrat smiled. "I see you have kept your anger. At least you feel something, David."

David charged him, grabbing him by the throat. Behind them, two other men entered. Out of the corner of one eye, Dave made out Dr. Jamal. The doctor's face looked to be in shock at seeing his patient trying to kill his new boss.

"David, stop it!" he shouted, trying to tear him from Muskrat's throat. The other doctor, Dr. Barry, grabbed Dave by both legs. Together, they forced him to the floor while Muskrat got his breath back. A moment later, the acting head of Psychiatry continued the interview.

"Do you see, Bloom," Muskrat asked when he had recovered, "how wrong Doctor Jamal was to let you out?"

"It has nothing to do with him, you turd," David croaked. "I'm innocent of any crime."

Muskrat chuckled. "Oh, come now, David. You'd never hurt me. Now, let's continue. I can see by your behavior that you are psychotic. Also hyper-maniacal and grandiose. For those reasons, we have put you on antipsychotics again. This one is of a new recipe. It's made in Russia, in fact in Moskva, my old hometown. You see, I'm dual nationality, just like you. French and Russian as opposed to Irish-American."

Muskrat hit the elevator button. "That's it, Mr. Bloom. I've other patients to attend to." As the silver door opened, he turned to his colleagues. "Come with me, gentlemen. We'll let the nurse handle Mister Bloom."

When David looked up from the floor, he saw Muskrat wave a hand at his two fellow psychiatrists. Jamal and Barry crept into the elevator beside their boss as the ox of a nurse marched out. When the elevator doors closed and they were alone, the nurse grabbed Bloom by the throat. "Don't even think about escaping," the ox stated with a growl. "One word out of you, and I'll throw you out the window."

Dave lashed out, striking the ox in his face. The nurse only tightened his grip and pushed him toward the large hospital window. David realized that the ox would hurl him through the glass if he did not stop struggling, to fall three floors onto the hard concrete surface of the patient courtyard. Ox spun him around, dragging David down a stairwell. At the bottom, in the basement, bruised and bloody, Bloom was hurled back into the Seclusion room.

"Don't worry, Bloom," hissed the nurse. "Twenty-one days passes quickly. That's the amount of time you have between now and your first patient tribunal. We'll even get you a lawyer paid for by the government because we know you're broke. Of course, the guy who will be assigned to you, solicitor Greeny Larson, doesn't have a great law degree. He's a farmer by trade and makes part of his income by conveyancing property. God knows, his skills in the HSE and Involuntary Admission are perfect for you. Why? Because Larson doesn't have any experience. And when, after the tribunal doesn't let you out, what then? Muskrat and me, we'll have you by the arse for three more months, that's what. Then three more months and three more months and three moreand probably forever. Got it?"

Ox leaned closer to the sweating face of David Bloom. "Sleep well, Bloom."

Then he spit on David's face and kicked him in the ribs. David didn't have to go to sleep. He was unconscious. Blood poured from his nose, forming a quiet red puddle on the tiled floor which reflected the moonlight coming through the single wire-reinforced window.

Three days later, still in Seclusion, Dave was woken by a pail of water poured over his head.

"Muskrat wants to see you right now!" Ox shouted as Dave wiped his face. "Now get up! You're off to testify before a special tribunal held in honor of Mr. David Bloom. At least you didn't have to wait for twenty-one days."

Dave was marched down a long hallway, then up a flight of stairs to the first floor. When he entered the room, he was forced to put on a straitjacket. Bound not only by the jacket but also by strength and honor, David knew his testimony would affect not only his life, but also his need to find Dolores. He was placed in a low chair, forced to look up at Muskrat and his crew. To Dave, it was like a Hitchcock nightmare: three men wearing long blue robes stared down at him from a table placed high on special risers. Muskrat banged a gavel.

"Hear ye, hear ye! Let this special tribunal be in session. Today, one David Bloom's life hangs in the balance. Now who is first to testify?"

"I object!" Dave shouted. "Where is my lawyer! I demand a lawyer!"

"The victim will be silenced!" said Ox, who clapped a beefy hand over Bloom's mouth, forcing him to silence.

Muskrat shuffled some papers, then held up a long piece of yellow paper. "I have here exhibit A. Dr. Paul, Mister Bloom's previous psychiatrist from twenty years ago, came to the conclusion that the defendant should be confined to Seclusion for the rest of his life." He grinned down, his eyes sparkling like a rat's. "What do you say to that, Mr. Bloom?"

"But that wasn't Dr. Jamal's conclusion." David gagged. "Jamal let me out because I no longer have verifiable symptoms of madness." Ox's grip tightened, again forcing the defendant into silence. He put his huge paws on David's throat, constricting the airway so that Dave could no longer talk.

"Silence in the courtroom!" Muskrat shouted. The man to his right leaned over, and Dave could hear him whisper to Dr. Muskrat that this was not a courtroom but a special sitting of a patient tribunal. Muskrat cleared his hairy throat and started over again.

"As I was sayingI agree with Dr. Paul's assessment, but I don't think he went far enough. The ruling of this court" Both men at Muskrat's sides looked askance at him. "Or should I say, tribunal, is the following. On count one: insanity in the first degree. We find him guilty! On count two: psychosis in the eternal degree: We find him guilty! And on the third count, and the most important—" Muskrat sniggered "—falling in love" He pretended to play a violin and sang as he swung an invisible bow. "When Autumn Leaves, Blow by the Window" He banged a gavel.

"GUILTY IN THE ONE MILLIONTH DEGREE. For being STUPID AND SILLY!" Muskrat again banged his black gavel. "This court is adjourned. But rather than twenty-one days until the next tribunal, we shall meet IN ONE YEAR at the same time and on the same channel—Bantry Psychiatric Unit Channel One! Dismissed! Bailiff, take the prisoner down!"

The Ox grabbed Bloom by the collar. He dragged him toward the door, but Dave pushed him off. With superhuman strength, he shook off the straitjacket.

"IF IT PLEASES THIS ILLEGAL COURT!" The room grew silent as David spoke. "What I'm doing isn't stupid or silly. I'm trying to find Dolores."

Muskrat sniggered. "Dolores Foley?" he squealed like a cast member from *Cats*. "Why, she must be a ghost because she died over twenty years ago."

"That's a lie! I know where she is."

"I'm so sorry, David. But as I said before, Carmel Foley is dead. Take the prisoner away," Muskrat sniffed. "Get him out of my sight!"

But Bloom wasn't done. He hoisted a heavy chair, smashing it over Ox's head, then leaped up onto the high table. He broke the chair across Muskrat's back, and then, using a broken chair leg, he fought with it like a saber. First, he slashed at one tribunal member's head, and then another. With superhuman strength, he leaped on Ox's back, beating him black and blue with his makeshift sword. Ox reached around David, who fought back like a fiend, and grabbed Dave by the arse. He threw David down, but Bloom stood up, charging him with every ounce of strength he had left. As he crashed into the oxen madman, Dave's body began to shudder. As he fell to the floor, he screamed one last time: "Dolores! Rachel! Help me beat these murderers!"

The door to the tribunal room flew open. Rachel strode in followed by their lawyer, Tony O'Brien. She saw her father on the floor and ran to him. "Someone call a doctor!"

She knelt, taking her father's bloody face in her hands. "Dad, wake up! Daddy?" At last, David opened his eyes, his daughter's sweet face coming into focus.

"Don't cry. I'm not going anywhere," he rasped. Then he coughed, blood spurting from his mouth and nose. As she watched, Rachel saw him close his eyes one last time as he embarked on his final journey.

"Dad, don't go. Oh, Daddy, my daddy. Please. Don't leave me alone here."

On the other side of the room, Dr. Muskrat got up, staggering, and called for his ox. But Ox lay dead on the floor, impaled by David's last stroke with his saber made from a wooden chair.

Then the room sparkled with ethereal light. The psychiatrist gazed up as a woman with long auburn hair and twinkling hazel eyes suddenly appeared. She floated like an angel toward Muskrat and his fellow tribunal members, all out to murder her husband, and slapped the psychiatrist across his face.

"Leave him alone!" Dolores cried, and turned to address the small audience. "You think him a monster, but after all, David is a human being just like you. A man filled with love and hope, anger and despair, joy and darkness. If you had not hunted him down and made him suffer, as a married couple, we would have only known a life of happiness. Yet you want us to know only heartbreak. Now leave him be!"

Muskrat smiled. "Happiness?" he sniggered. He leaped off the table, grabbing David's wooden saber. As she watched, horrified, he ran toward Rachel and she was certain he would impale her through the heart.

Like a fairy queen, Dolores soared high through the air, grasping Muskrat by the hair. She pulled the saber from his hand and then streaked to Ox, who lay dead on the floor, placing her glowing face on his dark heart. Breathing in, she sucked in the evil darkness deep within him. From the soul of the bloodied lout, dark squirming eels swarmed out of him like a swarm of locusts. The cancer rose in darkness and then descended, pouring into the mouths and then down the throats of Muskrat and the two other tribunal members. When it was finished, the three staggered toward the third-floor window. The window broke in long shards of glass, impaling the three monsters like Sinbad did when he killed the one-eyed Centaur. Then they fell, disappearing down a hole that had suddenly appeared, past a burning sign that read: The Gates of Hell.

When it was over, Dolores turned to Rachel and her lawyer.

"You have nothing to fear, either of you, because you are both as good as David, and better than almost all the others that live on this planet. Rest easy, both of you. Rachel, be gone. Go back to your husband because Jacob misses you."

With that, Dolores waved the saber that had been transformed into a magic wand. Rachel disappeared into thin air, the room buffeting from her departure.

"And as for you, my dear lawyer. I don't know you at all, but David told me your name is Tony. I'm sure you have a large family, and you're so good, Rachel would hardly have used you to defend her true love."

Then Dolores gazed out at you, our reader and audience, and stated:

"AND NOW, DEAR READER, IT'S TIME FOR THE
START OF OUR FINAL TWIST! Oh, you thought this was a
tale of heartbreak and happiness, did you? Well, you're wrong!
Because now, it's turning into a comedy so don't boo!"

Again, Dolores raised her wand, and the lawyer disappeared in a puff of smoke.

Then David rose (now out of character, writes the author) and stormed to Dolores: "As usual, Tony never had an opportunity to say one word"

"Wanna bet, dear audience?" Tony said on his exit, stage left: "This is a tragedy, Dolores, not a comedy! Now would you get off stage before Tom Richards, the author of this short story, throws you out!"

Dolores, who is played by Carmel Murray, Tom's saint and lover, said, "Tom and Tony, shut up for God's sake. Don't give the final twist away, or I'll just have to make love to both of you!" (Tony thought himself fortunate, but Tom wanted to kill Tony.)

"And so, dear reader, I'll let you in on the secret," said Tom, also known as David Bloom, to his audience. "This isn't a short story. It's actually a stage play that someday may be turned into a musical or a TV movie. And as to if it's fiction or not, well, that's up to you. Because as I write, Tom Richards is alive and well in room 5, Bantry Psychiatric Unit, just finishing rice pudding for dessert (and thinking of his new friend, Nurse Monica, who stars in *The Never-Ending Christmas*, elsewhere in this Anthology).

AND NOW FOR THE FINAL-FINAL TWIST:

Dolores, played by Carmel, took a deep breath to get back into character. She looked down at Tom, who again played David, as he closed his eyes and also took one deep breath.

"Oh, David, the love of my life, my beautiful man, my everything. My lover. My friend"

"Would you shut it, Dolores! Don't ham it up. That's not even in the script!"

Carmel shook out her arms and craned her neck back to relax, and started all over again. First, she turned to the prompter (played by Dr. O'Sullivan, psychiatrist, Bantry Psychiatric Clinic) and again ran through her lines. "Okay, I've got it," Carmel said, and dropped seamlessly back into character.

"It's time to leave, David, on our final voyage," Carmel whispered. "Come with me, you love of my life, and we'll make love forever."

MUSIC UP—"THE VOYAGE" BY
CHRISTY MOORE FOLLOWED
BY "WHEN I FEEL YOUR LOVE" BY ADELE

Dolores took David's hand and breathed into his mouth, restoring his life with one single breath. Then the room filled with glorious light as Dolores helped David up. And like Lazarus being raised from the dead, Dave stood up on two strong feet as if he was never dead.

`"Never again will you go through this tragedy," Dolores intoned. "Instead, we'll both act in a comedy and be happy forevermore, which is as life should be."

With that, the bright light grew and song filled the room like a heavenly choir. He took her hand, and together they leaped through a glowing circle of golden light. A BOOM like a clap of thunder and— they were gone!

AUDIENCE—APPLAUSE!

"Wait! Wait!" shouted friend Frank, who played Muskrat, with a wig and whiskers on his egg-shaped head. "The play isn't over! There's

113

one more scene to go. Now would you feckin change the scenery, please, before I shout: "EGGS FOR EVERYONE!"

(ENTER STAGEHANDS WHO CHANGE THE STAGE BACK TO THE SECLUSION ROOM)

Muskrat, aka Frank, stood stock-still, staring at a wall and braying like a donkey at a full moon that suddenly appeared through the reinforced single window.

"What's wrong with him?" Dolores, also known as Carmel, asked, now playing Monica, the psychiatric nurse. "Didn't Muskrat get his feed sack today?"

"Not that I know of," said Tom, now playing the dolphin for the movie, *Dolphin Song*. Dressed like a black-and-white common dolphin, with a spotted white face, Tom sported a large fin on his back and a single pair of flippers on his feet. He slipped, and Frank aka Muskrat, who was supposed to be comatose, caught him.

"That's out of character, Frank," Tom shouted, because he was also the director. "But to answer Carm's question," he stated, getting back into character, "damned if I know. With any luck, Frank, the egg man will be hauling eggs forever."

LIGHTS DOWN. APPLAUSE. LIGHTS
UP. ALL CAST MEMBERS BOW

The Cast of Characters
Frank: Muskrat
Carmel Murray: Dolores
Tom Richards: David Bloom
Ox: Noel Forde, Keiran Lyons (Understudy)
Dr. Jamal: Played by himself, with coaching from Doctor O'Sullivan
David Bloom's lawyer: Tony O'Brien
Psychiatric nurse Monica: played by Bantry Psychiatric Unit nurse
Monica

Nurses and staff: real-life members of Bantry
Psychiatric Unit, Bantry County Cork, Ireland
Tribunal judges: Lawrence Wilson & Stan Hayes
Script by: Tom Richards and Carmel Murray,
super-angels and long-lost lovers
With inspiration from: Romeo and Juliet
Music courtesy of: Christy Moore & Adele
Scenery, stage construction, and lighting by:
Robert Smith, RIP, Illinois Wesleyan
University graduate
Production manager/sword play choreography:
Alison Vesley, RIP, Illinois Wesleyan
University graduate
Completed this day: 9:30 a.m., April 4, 2022,
while Tom is still an involuntary patient at
the above-named psychiatric unit

MORE APPLAUSE FROM AUDIENCE. LIGHTS UP

ALARUM! ALARUM!

Frank steps out, still dressed as Muskrat.

"Good news for everyone! When you buy a copy of *Always Come Home*, the full novel (go to www.tomrichards.ie), you get— FREE OFFER!—ONE DOZEN EGGS FROM THE EGG MAN! Unfortunately, participating markets only include the Bantry Psychiatric Unit, Bantry, County Cork, Ireland, and then on Tuesdays in even-numbered years only."

With that, the audience throws raw eggs at Frank. Two dozen hit him in the face. SPLAT SPLAT SPLAT
– THE END –

Note: Solicitor Tony O'Brien is, in real life, my lawyer. And it is a fact that, as I type, it is 1100 hrs on April 4, 2022. In three hours, I have a hearing before Ireland's High Court. At that time, I shall be judged innocent of all charges. I'm outta this Unit due to two factors.

First, I note the following article of Ireland's Constitution, which guarantees our right to freedom and which will be used by my lawyer to justify my release from involuntary admission to this psychiatric unit:

> Article 40.4.2° Upon complaint being made by or on behalf of any person to the High Court or any judge thereof alleging that such person is being unlawfully detained, the High Court and any and every judge thereof to whom such complaint is made shall forthwith enquire into the said complaint and may order the person in whose custody such person is detained to produce the body of such person before the High Court on a named day and to certify in writing the grounds of his detention, and the High Court shall, upon the body of such person being produced before that Court and after giving the person in whose custody he is detained an opportunity of justifying the detention, order the release of such person from such detention unless satisfied that he is being detained in accordance with the law.

My pending freedom is also due to a sudden change in attitude by a psychiatrist named Muskrat who is worried that the above hearing will set a precedent and that he'll be fired forthwith!

Whatever happens, and following a physical (completed at the State of Ireland's expense: value well over $1,500 if held in the US or so I'm told) I'M OUTTA HERE IN THE MORNING! Thanks for reading. Manâna, and talk to you later—Tom

Copyright 2022, Storylines Entertainment Ltd. For all rights, or to sell Frank's eggs on contract for a very small profit, contact Tom Richards at tomrichards141@gmail.com. See www.tomrichards.ie for more information.

A Very Short Story And Collection of Poetry by Will Arnold

Equinox

"That's it, I've had it!"

"Well don't you think I've had it too?! I'm gonna –"

"You're going to put on your shoes and go for a drive with me. Right now!"

I smoldered while she drove. I had no idea where she was going. "Overall, you've been a good husband and we made a good kid together but now –"

"Now you're just going to dump me in the drink, is that it?" I eyed the Chicago River to my right as we sped along. At a red light she turned to look at me through her sunglasses.

"You poor little boy," she sighed. Then she smiled. Sort of. "After a break-up, what a man loses in a woman he can never find within himself."

She hit the gas, knocking me into the trunk. "But a woman is delighted to finally reveal things in herself she suppressed for too long." We screeched to a stop.

"Here! Now get out." We walked to Millennium Park and she hailed a dark-haired woman reflected by The Bean. "Are you Loretta?" The woman nodded pleasantly.

"What IS all of this?"

"THIS is your second wife, Loretta. And if you'd been smart, you'd have married her first! I'm keeping the car and the condo. Good bye!"

"Hello, Ray! You're too thick in the paunch and too light on top but I think we'll make do for each other nicely!" Loretta had an oblate face but her teeth were good and her thick wavy black hair set off her blue eyes quite nicely. She had saddle-bag thighs but friendly breasts.

She interlaced her arm with mine and guided me towards the summer crowd, all in heat. I stopped.

"Wait. I don't know but I need to know. Am I heartbroken that I am out of her life or am I happy that she is out of mine? I don't know and I *need* to know. Maybe I'm both. Or neither. What do you think, Loretta?" Loretta poked my nose with her index finger. She smiled and said, "Yes."

Automat (after Edward Hopper)

So beautiful, half of her lovers might exclaim

So troubled, the rest of them would observe

Clean table, white as hospital bed. Chair

Opposite mocking in its emptiness

In a voice of papier-mache fruit and flowers. "Darling,

Aren't the lights overhead like parallel fates

That emerge and fade into the double-glassed pane

To keep us warm while we might sip our tea?

What if those lights are ours? Perhaps, if we are good,

They will converge as one upon our horizon."

No cream, no sugar for her tea. The War. It does not matter.

The heel of silk stocking melted by dancing

(A cup of tea only a nickel at the Automat)

With him in joy and champagne before his gray

And green departed for night, his plane overhead

Runway lights ascending into night, her tea's chill.

So beautiful she is, facing vacant chair. Back to window.

Twin reflected lights in cup recede into memory.

At Night's End

Alchemy. What love makes of rain-soaked roots

Your body dark matter of mud and feather

I do not know which shape is shadow or

Stillness of wind. Deeper than lock, league or loom

Babies in the eyes. Curved space of orbit --

And you, and only you, at the crescent of night's end, keep

Better places for my being when it loves you.

Sheathed and unsheathed, paper costumes of no mask

 Consume with fire in arc on chord; dune of sand

And sidewinder our sin and heaven

Protest only if we cannot go together.

In the image of you but not your likeness --

Lay your body down to all points, your hands

Towards water. All origins. All destinations.

We awaken to smear and blur of ghost train

Pressed together at God's thinning hairline

Of the dawn, naked and multiple

Emerge from sweat effigies cleaved and clamped –

The hinge bends to keep us part in piece

We surrender to survive; we cannot go back

Only take the train to fulfill our circle.

Chamber Music

Quintet for Oboe and Lover

Arc of spell, roseleaf tide

Half-moon of her belly in jewels and August.

Neck of lightning. It has not changed.

Lemon slice of her foot, cunning scythe

Whirled by madman to paint his circus cell

Looking Glass Writing. Read the mirror.

A dory lay at harbour in bloom midnight

Murmur meringue crescents

Lap of ice cream stitching dark skin

Matryoshka doll, layers of ocean

Giving endless birth to herself

Creaking door in baby's cry. It will not change.

Gather refugee pieces in ripped burlap bag

In miniatures while evening naps.

Milkweed will flow from ripe open wound

In coda.

The Burning Woman

If only a woman had created God,

As lover and not keeper. Salvation

As they move to make love with earth

Syncopation of drone insects.

Cooling shade from a burning woman

Where he might find redemption in her

And not in what he has made of her

To repair her boat, rub salve on her feet

She wanted only a safe way home.

When God fell in love and offered to her

Ghosts and bones tossed to the lightning seas

Blue notes in lullabies for soldiers and psalms. He meant well

And she forgave him. Women of love

Wear their haloes around unbowed necks

Spirits disguised in myth, scents of night --

What could he possibly say to her?

A woman in love sings

Alone to her heart, washless tide; bones

Of folded gull wing found on steps of shore

Spent sonnets whisper ash to night

From fires that hermits attend.

Perfect Center

Conjure Woman, she became of him a Linden

Root, source and leaf – she reclined and dreamed

In his gift and blessing of shade.

She slept within his shape. He whispered to her moon arc

And phase and both lay down beneath water.

Naked frolic frozen in dusty snow globe

On bookshelf. All fingerprints wiped clean

No trace lingers of crime or criminals, they

Laugh down the street chased by priest

Cursing after them in Latin.

She took nothing but left little more,

What he found in her hands while she danced

When her eyes became his heartbeat --

Her leaves mattered so much to the boy

And now the boy is deepest root of the man.

The meaning of something moving.

Come, old one, to bed

Your feet are soft and perfect as bread

Your shoulders have forgiven the rain

After so many years and miles of journey.

The scent of the room was vanilla

Fresh rosemary in humid alcove where we planted candles

For our devotionals.

A ripeness of spice and scent

Secreted down into the apple cellar

Love survives as it is recalled in winter solstice

The frozen saints. But little more. Two are two.

Come, old one, to bed.

How sad we cannot keep our memories of snow

Together. How they differ in recall, how different

We must have been, even then.

How sad we do not share the memory of snow as one;

Love, womb of antique angels,

Does not care how wide a lifetime can become.

The bed of youth now not big enough

Where we dream together of other places

Love survives as it is recalled in ritual harvest

The apple cellar. Your feet on stairs. Two are two.

Come, old one, to bed.

Bride from Birth

Heavy with light
    Bride from birth
        Barefoot child on checked floor
Chords of clock smear. Tones blur. Love dances.

    Light drips from ledge to bless
        Yellow bear in sundress
    Book for master, pen from mistress

She returns to her story
    He to his craft of sea journey
        Wave and wash of winds, one in nightfall
Caught hearts, free whisper plainsong. Night is all.

    She reclines like a star only for him
        Strike of silver drum in precision
    Chime of crystal string in rhythm

She has recalled her mystery
    He plays diamond-patched Harlequin
        Scatter of cat claws across wood
Chant candle. Sudden beat two. Sea is dry.

    Corners of cut glass, her facets reflect
        Arcs and pulses, resonant tensile strength,

The loving heart is ripely cleft.

Winter Follows

She might see him
When she cuts her leg shaving in August --
        She might draw herself cartoon
    Of sexy blood-red moon
She daubs at each sacrificial drop
       "She loves me, she loves me not"

    She might see me in a single rose petal
        I am in her, I am always in her
    Even as she bleeds me out in summer.

Radio on
Bathing baby in back room
Inhabited by ghost of body
Moist halo of calloused footfall.

Radio on
Clown in haunted house, each comic
Terror is her eyes in his bag of marbles
Cleansed of youth and attic dust --

It will melt in sweat effigies from them.
Winter follows.

The Switchman

Lantern in the fog, kerosene-scented breeze
    Grease-striped overalls. Polished silver watch in pocket.
        Thin as rain, a spot on the map

Dried whiskey or fresh blood, the stitching spreads
    Grime of night in deep creases of palm; fine
        Veins of muscled hands grip steel lever

Of train yard change of fire. Switchman
    Grinning in the gloaming, mail-hook gibbet
        Of county station. Resembling scaffold.

Hoboes yawn and rise from straw
    Smeared with cow-car shit and emerge
    From egg shells; sea turtles freshly born
Scurry to safe sea from sand predators.

The Intended (after Conrad's *Heart of Darkness*)

It did not seem fair to touch her – unfair
To touch her white hand carved from night, to
Stand before her, Misbegotten Lucifer.

    His last word – to live with, she insisted. I loved him

Our words were fire and ash, Jacob's Ladder

Angels ascending, devils descending curtains,

Dead groom's grimace wide in the valance.

The last word he pronounced was -- your name.

Transfigured swan. She became her own myth.
Albatross circling unreal sky. Rain washes out his grave.
Heaven is God's lie, love, a woman's --

I knew it – I was sure!

"His bed now black and deep as our slumber
        His sleep soon overspilled with white bones,
            Now the red sun can break us no more.

"His end has come, now mine can begin. Maid
        And martyr of stained glass. Love is perfect for two
Only when one of them is dead."

A pencil journey

Glad remembrance. A curl of deception
Crumbled wing of a thinking bird.
The humid green dies, dries
And confesses its secret,
Possum shadows mimic gypsy clouds –
Hold a fire in your hands
See what patience you have left.

Nude bathers on a bookshelf
Their ripples are poetry
Missions of disbanding hell swarm;
Light crystals in fiery corsage
Lightning in night's orgasm. The

Dance dissolves all unpolished edges --
A perfect apple reminds me of you
October ovals, taste before hunger,
All of the love, in surrendered piety,
Raises me to caress one bit of truth.

Shedding your skin before snowlight pool
Blue Witch, bones of wings chant in trees
Blossoms hushed, abandoned, awaiting
Widened nights to harvest thick fragrance --
Art cannot portray the same
Beautiful impulse of muscle or
Instinct of passion
That a child needs to live.

Until there was only one

March sun made his conquests upon the snowmen
Melted two for breakfast, a third for lunch
Had another for snack with hot chocolate
Until there was only one

Summer night washed pastel chalks with rain
Poured all the children's paintings to the street
Came to end of your avenue, busked cello
Until there was only one

Winter noon blew all the leaves away into white
Stuck all the trees to blue and gray palettes
Paused to watch a football game then crashed
Until there was only one

Autumn twilight bathed the day in deep ruby glow

Sang a song for lovers or those almost in love
Watched as we courted our flames together
Until there was only one.

About Will Arnold
Poet and Short-story writer, Will Arnold, lives in Chicago, Illinois. He has published three volumes of poetry and short fiction: **Arlington Horizons, Ghost Serenades** and **The Late Movie**. For more information, contact the author: worldinall1119@comcast.net and to purchase his books, please go to his author's page: https://www.amazon.com/Will-Arnold/e/B00ZF3FRWS

Redemption Invictus

By
Helen Rowntree Edited and co-authored by Tom Richards
Based on the true incident experienced by
Alison McCarthy* (not her real name)

In a poorer area of Cork's inner city, located in southern Ireland, high up in a squalid set of flats, Alison McCarthy sits at her Formica kitchen table stirring milk into a hot cup of tea. Her long, black, straight hair droops to the table, dull in the morning sunlight that streams through the closed windows as her young face, lined with worry, studies yet another overdue rent bill. When she notes the kind note from her landlord, Tom Roberts, stapled to the bill, she smiles. His neat capital letters spell out the words, ALISON, DON'T WORRY ABOUT THIS MONTH'S RENT. IT CAN WAIT. TOM. Yet as her puffy eyes move to a pile of other unpaid bills, she realizes that she *does* worry about it and will continue to until she's completely caught up with her overdue creditors.

She starts hacking, a cough that won't stop. Running to her small bathroom, she looks in the mirror. Her eyes are red from a persistent flu, her cheeks aflame from a small fever. Alison opens her medicine cabinet. There's nothing in there except an empty box of aspirin she used during the last time she got sick. She remembered how she had to go to the doctor, paying twenty euro for the small prescription of twelve tablets. But now they were gone and she couldn't afford another script from her local GP.

Walking back into the kitchen, still coughing, she can see her three children in the front living room—Tim, a three-year-old toddler, and twins Siobhan and Gloria, both one-year-olds—lie asleep on the couch which also serves as their bed when the bottom is pulled out. The small flat is impeccable. As the children nap, Alison cleans the room top to bottom, as well as the small toilet with its sink and shower, and her small kitchen. She has three part-time jobs and somehow, despite her lack of sleep due to getting up to breastfeed the twins at eleven, two, and five o'clock in the morning before walking briskly to her first job, Alison also cooks and manages to attend night school for her bachelor's degree in engineering. Smart, funny, skilled, and practical, Alison also has an interest in mathematics as well as helping to raise money for a single-parents charity.

Tonight, it's a different story as Alison, overwhelmed by the money she owes, struggles to make ends meet yet again.

Her monthly rent is two-hundred and fifty euro per week, a little more than the weekly single mother's allowance the government pays directly into her bank account. As it is, she must work at those three small jobs (one in a small local grocery store, one in a restaurant as a waitress, and the final one at her university as a guest lecturer in engineering, though she earns very little cash per teaching class), making enough money to feed the kids, buy nappies, and pay for electricity and other essentials. Needless to say, she just gets by.

She glances at her mobile phone. It's just past six in the morning and she knows it's time to get moving. But first she decides to check her online BAI Bank account to see if her single mother's allowance has come into her current account. The payment, just over two-hundred euro a week, helps significantly with the rent. But when she tries to log in, she finds that she can't. Over and over again, her thumbs enter the five numbers that are also the birthdays of her family so she won't forget.

"That can't be wrong!" she whispers so as not to wake the kids. Her eyes narrow as she concentrates yet again to type in the numbers that are her financial lifeline. "Five is little Tim's birthday. Seven and seven. That's Grace and Gloria's birthday. Then my husband Pookey's birthday is last: Twenty." She still can't get into her online bank account.

Alison picks up her bag that hangs on a chair and takes out her purse. Looking through it, she sees only a single five euro note and some change. It's enough to buy milk for Timmy, but she can forget the rent and any of the other bills that are due. Quietly, making sure she doesn't wake the kids, Alison puts on her thick duffel coat, lets herself out the front door, and inches down the hall so as not to wake the apartment's other families so early in the morning. Outside, she finds the weather cold and brisk. The sun has not yet risen because it's midwinter, and she breaks into a trot, heading down the empty streets, past parked cars that glitter with early morning frost to the nearest BAI Branch, which is located just down the street.

"At least the ATM machine is working for a change," she mutters, thinking how often it's not. The bright green light winks merrily at her as if inviting her to a gift of free money. Alison pushes her cashcard into the glowing slot and punches in those precious five numbers. The glass of the machine glows as the mechanisms chunts. Then a message appears: TRANSACTION DECLINED. It gives no reason.

Now angry, Alison again tries her five numbers. When that doesn't work, she searches her wallet for a BAI Visa Card. Pulling the cashcard from the machine, she inserts the other card. The numbers are the same but in reverse: 2 0 7 7 5.

Once again, the ATM hums and chunts. Yet the message is the same: TRANSACTION DECLINED.

"But there's money in *both* accounts!" she hisses, her warm breath turning to mist in the cold, glowing in the soft lights of the streetlamps. "I know there is. There's at least two-hundred and forty euro in my current account. And I had a zero balance on my Visa Card. I have a five-hundred-euro line of credit. So I should be able to pull at least two-hundred and seventy euro from that card."

Alison wanted to pay Tom his rent while also buying some food for the day. The denial of her Visa card was particularly infuriating. She rarely used it, only for emergencies, and always kept the balance at zero. There was no reason in the world why her card should be denied.

Alison looks across the street, seeing a SuperValu sign glowing in the early morning darkness. She realizes she could buy the milk for Tim and get some cash back at the checkout counter at the same time. But when she finishes shopping and presents her cards to the woman at the register, first the cash card and then the Visa credit card, the store employee, Eva, a close friend, looks up at her in embarrassment and smiles in sympathy.

"Alison, I'm sorry, but both cards have been declined. It's happened to me before. It's terrible, isn't it?"

"But that's not right!" states Alison. "I have money in both accounts. How could they be declined?"

Eva studies the half liter of milk Alison is carrying. "Have you ever been hacked?" Eva asks. "I have, and it is absolutely horrible! It took me weeks to clear it up. Go to the bank as soon as you can. If you need to, cancel both cards and have them reissue you new ones with brand-new numbers. It's the only way to make certain your money is safe."

"I know about hacking," Alison says. "I've read all about it. But BAI has one of the most secure antihacking software systems in the world. Idiots like hacking criminals could not possibly have stolen my money."

"Are you sure, Alison? BAI isn't that clever. I read somewhere that they've been hacked numerous times in the recent past. Wasn't Ireland's major financial institution, Bank of Old Ireland, hacked successfully? And they're supposed to have a track record that's one of the best in the world."

Alison ends up buying the milk with her small change, then leaves the store. As she walks out the front door, she feels the cold bite her face.

"Why does it always feel colder just before dawn?" she asks herself, seeing the glimmer of sunlight on the clouds sweeping in from the nearby Atlantic. Then she pulls her coat tight and trots back to the flat. As she opens the door, she knows that she will be at the bank at ten o'clock, just when it opens. She will have to take a few minutes off from her job at the grocers, but knows she can clear up the mess in seconds. After all, it's all been a mistake. She'll talk to Brian, the branch manager, if she has a problem with the bank teller. He'll solve it in no time. After all, she considers him a close acquaintance. He'd had her over to his mansion of a house in Ballincollig, a leafy Cork City suburb, for her birthday. It was only when he made an unwelcome advance that her opinion changed. "Alison, I'm smitten, don't you know that?" Brian had said in an awkward attempt at an explanation.

As she backed away from him, Alison reminded Brian of one important fact. "Brian, for Chrissake. I'm married. How many times have you met my Pookey, the nickname for my husband John? You know he's in the hospital with Early Onset Alzheimer's."

It was only when Brian's face turned bright red that she realized he did remember but didn't give a damn. Brian was only trying to get what he wanted, and that was sex. Nothing more. Turning, she ran all the way back to her flat to be with her children and her best friend Sally. Alison considered closing her BAI Bank account but felt that Brian had only made a mistake. She remembered that he had lost his partner, Jill, five months earlier. After all, when people are grieving, they get lonely and often make mistakes or suffer from poor judgment, they're so upset.

Writing it off as a bad experience, Alison forgave Brian and vowed to give him another chance.

But now, a few months after that terrible experience, with midwinter approaching, and thinking she had been hacked by an online criminal gang, she realizes she is going crazy. Having made it home from SuperValu with her liter of milk, she studies her change purse again and begins to realize the financial jam she is in. Taking out her notebook, she begins to tally up what she couldn't pay: her heat (which isn't included in the rent) or the monthly bills for her mobile phone and online Wi-Fi services. Thinking she did something wrong, she calls the BAI Bank customer services 1-800 phone number but is first put on hold for forty-five minutes. When the nice man finally answers, she is interrupted by her twins screaming with hunger.

"I need to replace both of my cards," she cries to the man as the children scream. "It must have been something I did because my cards don't work *anywhere*, and I need to get food and heat, and pay my rent."

"No, it's not you," replies the pleasant customer services rep as he checks his computer. "My data shows that your cards are alive and well and haven't been used in awhile. Particularly the Visa card, which shows a zero balance. Honestly, they should both work anywhere you present them. If I were you, I'd talk to your bank manager to see if he can discover what's wrong."

When she hangs up, she remembers that she gave her son Tim a banana for breakfast, and a mashed banana for the twins. But now poor

Alison remembers she is out of almost everything else. Opening the fridge, she sees only the plastic milk bottle she bought and one small cup of yogurt. Reaching up and opening the cupboards, she finds they contain only two cans of soup.

Telling Tim to mind the twins for a minute, she crosses the narrow hallway to her best friend's apartment. When the door opens, Sally listens as behind her a roomful of children wail.

"Sally, can you mind my kids for a few minutes? I just have to go to the bank and shouldn't be too long," Alison shouts to make herself heard above the din.

"What's wrong, Alison?" Sally asks, noting her neighbour's tear-streaked face.

"It's just a small problem. I did something wrong when I tried to bank online, and now nothing is working. I'm sure this won't take too long for Brian, the bank manager, to fix."

When Sally agrees, Alison finds that once again she is back on the street, now walking through freezing rain and wind to the bank. At the branch, the lobby is practically empty because the branch has just opened. When she sees her branch manager, Brian, she tries to explain what happened. But instead, Brian starts to scream at her, startling Alison half to death.

"We know what you did! The lobby CCTV camera caught you making huge withdrawals and transferring the money overseas to buy some kind of house in Florida as well as an investment property in Spain. Where are you getting that kind of money? Are you one of those tricksters approaching old ladies and committing fraud? Alison, I've called the Garda Síochána at the local police station. I've reported you for theft, and I'm sure you'll go to jail for the next forty years! We have records showing that those transfers," he states, pointing to the green blinking light of the BAI overseas transfer machine, "have exceeded €1,500,000! Yet nothing has come out of your current account, and that's all the proof I need to show that you're stealing! You must be taking it from someone else's account. That's pretty clever. You're studying engineering and I bet you study computer code as part of your course."

"Brian," Alison pleads, "keep your voice down. Yes, we study computers but CAD design, not computer coding. You know I'm worth practically nothing. I live day by day and have only a fiver in my pocket. See?" Alison pulls a ragged five euro note from her tattered bag. "You know I'm taking night classes in engineering to get a good-paying job and more income. Where's your proof, Brian? Did you ever see me using that crazy machine?" Alison points at the foreign transaction machine. "Did you really take pictures of me doing it or was it someone else? I've *never* used that damned machine. See the CCTV?" she states firmly, pointing at a camera positioned in the corner of the room that looks down on them. "Show me the footage of me using that bloody machine."

Brian looks at the floor, realizing he'd better have proof at hand before he accuses anyone of theft again, and reconsiders his accusation. "I'm sorry, Alison. Just watch what you're doing when you're banking here, okay? Don't go near that transfer machine without my permission."

"Who the hell do you think I am," Alison snaps. "I'm a customer, aren't I? Don't you dare accuse me of anything again." She takes a step back from him, calming down. "Let's forget about it, okay? Brian, look. About my engineering course. I want to get a loan from BAI Bank. In fact, while I'm here, can you give me a personal loan application? All I need is seven-hundred and fifty euro for next year's class."

"We don't keep the forms in the branch," Brian explains. "Today, everything is online. Download the application form, fill it in and sign it, bring it back in, and I'll process your request." But Alison knows by the look on his face that he will always deny her the small personal loan because of the grudge he has against her for refusing him sex.

"Okay, I'll download the form, print it and bring it in," she lies because she can't afford a printer and doesn't own one. "Brian, while I'm here, I want to withdraw this week's social welfare payment of two-hundred and fifty euro. I need it to feed the kids and heat the flat."

"Two-fifty, is that what you want?" Brian states, his eyes narrowing as he again thinks of the substantial hacking. He has already reported the theft to the bank's head office. It was for that reason Alison's account is frozen, not that she knows he ordered it. Thinking quick, he makes a management decision.

"How about fifty euro to tide you over until next week? During that time, I'll work hard to clear up this mess you're in." He studies her eyes, stepping closer. "Why are your eyes so red? And I swear, you've been drinking and it's only ten o'clock in the morning. Don't lie because I can smell it from here. Alison, are you in that kind of trouble? Are you an alcoholic?"

Alison's cheeks turn red at this second false accusation. "For God's sake, Brian. My personal life is none of your bloody business. And if it makes any difference, no I'm not an alcoholic."

"Of course, you're not," he says smiling and decides he'd better come clean with this crazy woman. "Look, you'd better know the truth. I've already reported you for theft. We'll launch an investigation to prove if the accusation is true and that's a promise. But in the meantime, your accounts stay frozen."

"You talk about proving if the accusation is true?" she says in a loud voice. "You've frozen my account and cards and you don't even have proof yet? Brian, I need my money. It's my property."

"Is it your property or someone else's?" he asks, his voice brittle. He crosses his arms, his face turning serious. "I talked to my boss this morning. We need a letter from your solicitor proving to us that you're not an alcoholic. Alcoholics lie and steal. You'll have to go to your doctor to take a blood test first. Maybe it's true that you're not an alcoholic. Maybe you're on cocaine. It has the same symptoms. At the same time as you do that, we'll look through every transaction across the entire branch network. If we can prove that you didn't do it, then we'll unfreeze your accounts.

"Prove that I didn't do it?" she retorts. "What happened to being considered innocent until proven guilty? You don't have proof so unlock my account! I'm absolutely clean. Brian, I've taken nothing this morning or last night. Not a drink or a tablet. Nothing at all."

"Haven't you? I've known you for years and your behaviour this morning is uncharacteristic. Alison, I'm sorry, but I've seen you stumbling when you came into the lobby and you've been slurring your words as we've talked."

Alison knows the last part of Brian's speech to be true. She had the flu for a week, and she was snorting and stumbling due to her fever. Her eyes were red not only from being sick but also from Brian's unwelcome lecture and her unsettled morning.

"I'm *not* crazy enough to snort coke or drink a lot," Alison states, trying to sound reasonable. She clears her throat, trying not to cough. "I'm only upset and sick with flu. Wouldn't you be if you were told you needed a letter to prove your innocence? Brian," Alison pleads, "how can I get a solicitor? I can't afford anything, and now you want me to hire a lawyer?"

"That's *your* problem, not mine," Brian states. "Now please leave the branch or I'll be forced to call the Gards, telling them that you're causing a disturbance."

Outside the branch, Alison crouches in the cold and begins to sob her eyes out. It takes what seems like an hour to stop. Wiping her eyes and getting up on unsteady legs, she feels the plight of any of those who are broke and near homeless. She has next to nothing. She knows her young family will be tossed out of the flat because she will be unable to pay the rent, which is due in a day. Now, a week before Christmas, she can hear the bells of a local church toll and sees the bright lights in the window of Mary's Shop, a local store where Alison often buys groceries on the tick. The small balance is overdue, too, and Alison knows that Mary, while patient, cannot afford her overdue payments any longer.

Then Alison sees a local Saint Vincent de Paul sergeant march down the street. Behind the old woman is a small marching band, all dressed in SVP yellow-and-blue uniforms. One soldier clangs a bell looking for donations to feed the poor. When the old sergeant sees Alison, her eyes full of tears, she orders her small troop to halt.

"Are you okay, child?" the old woman asks, taking Alison's arm to steady her. "You look hungry and upset. Come in out of the cold. Our local SVP shop is right down the street. We've hot soup on the cooker and it's ready to be served up. So dry your tears, and I'll listen carefully while you get something to eat."

At the small SVP store, Alison is served soup with bread and butter, and eats and talks while the woman, who introduces herself as Maggie, listens intently. As she hears Alison's financial difficulties and the fact that her kids are hungry and she can't keep the flat warm or pay her bills, the old soldier is horrified. Then Alison tells Maggie about Brian and his impossible accusations.

"He won't help you?" When Alison again breaks down, both elbows on the table as she sobs her heart out, Maggie strokes the young woman's long hair. "You stay here and finish your meal. I'll be right back."

Alison watches as the old woman confers with a group of other SVP volunteers. When the sergeant comes back, she's clutching a small white envelope which she hands to the stricken young woman. But Alison pulls back.

"Go on. Take it."

"What's in it?"

"Only a small gift. Call it an early Christmas present. Go on, child. It's for your kids."

When Alison finishes her soup and bread, she walks out the front door, giving her thanks to Maggie and the other women. She sits on a bench, sunning herself in the growing morning light. Opening the envelope, she pulls out some notes, counting two hundred and fifty euro. It is enough to pay Tom and buy a bit more food. She glances back at the SVP shop. A line of homeless has gathered at the front door for lunch. Thinking that someday she will repay the volunteers and SVP for their kindness, Alison gets up from the bench and heads back to the bank more determined than ever to straighten things out.

The lobby is crowded because it's just after noon and the bank closes for lunch at one o'clock. Finding Brian in his office, she again pleads her case. Once again, he lectures her, stating that he will call the Gards and reaches for the phone on his desk. Alison backpedals into the lobby, past friends and neighbors from her apartment block. She startles, stumbling, when seeing a full professor from her university making a withdrawal from the teller.

"I did what I promised," Brian shouts, having followed Alison into the lobby. "The Gards are on the way and you could well be arrested. You'll be frog-marched out of here and if found guilty of fraud, and if I had my way, you'd never be let out of prison."

Glancing toward the professor, Alison notices the mature man's confused face. Then his brow furrows as he comes to his own conclusion based on nothing but Brian's false words. As Alison hurries once again from the lobby, she knows that her reputation is in ruins. Not only do her friends and neighbors think she's a fraudster, but the professor does too. With her bad luck he'll tell his colleagues, who will pass on the misinformation to her head of department. That woman, Ann Carroll, is also her PhD sponsor and evaluator. In one fell swoop, Brian might have destroyed Alison's career.

Back at the flat, and after having another cup of tea to calm herself and checking on her kids, she walks downstairs where she gives Tom the rent. All he does is shake his head and hold up both hands.

"Alison, I'm sorry, but Mrs. Birdcamp, a neighbor on your floor, was in the bank and heard the commotion as Brian ordered you out. You know that I'd love to keep you here as a tenant. But I'm afraid you don't have a lease, as you know. Too, Mrs. Birdcamp told me you were behaving insanely, and if that's true, if you are an alcoholic and mentally incompetent, you can't sign a lease or any type of contract, or even keep the flat for another month because that's a verbal contract. If you default again on your rent, and can't pay anything in the future, don't you see I'll lose my job?"

Alison can't believe his words. "Tom, I thought we were friends."

"We are! But I'm just like you. I have two little girls and a partner who depends on me. What are they going to do if I lose my job?"

Alison hangs her head as Tom continues, "Forgive me, but you'll have to pack your bags, find another place to live, and leave by 5:00 p.m. tonight. Those are management's rules, not mine. Do please keep in touch because I consider us the greatest of friends. I'm just sorry I can't help you and the kids anymore."

"Isn't there anything else you can do, Tom? Can't you just give me one more day to get this mess cleared up? You know I'm not insane or an alcoholic." Alison thrusts the cash that she still holds again at Tom. "Please, take this. It's all I've got."

Tom looks at the cash clutched in her hand and shakes his head yet again. "Alison, keep that. Seeing that you won't be living here anymore, the rent of course is not due at all." He shakes his head again and takes off his glasses. "If it's any comfort, I know you're telling the truth. You're sane and competent. In fact, you're one of the sanest people I've ever met."

***

At 5:00 p.m. exactly, Sally grasps the three-year-old's hand as Alison pushes her pram filled with her twins out the door of her apartment complex back into the cold. They stand for a moment in the small apartment lobby, looking out on the twilight, and both see it has begun to snow.

"Oh, Alison, I wish I could keep you and the kids in my flat. But you see, my sister Sarah is also in financial trouble, and you know that I am too. Do please remember that Sarah has four tiny children, and together with my own three tots, it's more than my small flat can hold. There simply aren't enough beds."

Sally tries to give Alison some money that she can't afford, but Alison only gives her a peck on the cheek.

"Keep your money, Sally. Me and the kids will be fine. I'm walking up the road to the Saint Vincent de Paul. Sister Maggie, I'm sure, can find us all somewhere to sleep tonight. She's such a kind woman, with a heart of pure gold. She listened when I was talking about what happened at the bank. See?" Alison goes on, holding out the cash Maggie gave to her but Tom refused. "It's enough to keep us going for at least two weeks if I stretch it." Then the friends hug again, and as tears sting Sally's eyes, Alison pushes her family out into the snow.

***

The SVP shop is crowded that night with families struggling to make ends meet. All require a hot meal to warm them from the winter's chill. When Alison comes into the shop, the first thing she does after brushing the snow off her children is to march to the kitchen.

"Is there anything I can do to help?" she asks the kitchen staff. "Many people are in so much more trouble than I am. I've always worked hard. If you can please give me a meal to feed the kids, I'd like to help you first, and then I'll eat."

The staff, always overworked, gaze back at her gratefully. "Thank you, dear," says an older volunteer, a woman with scaled red hands from cooking and cleaning too much. "If you could serve up bowls of lamb stew and add a piece of bread and butter, you can then serve them to the people out in the large hall. All they want to do is eat because, you're right, they're in trouble. Many are alcoholics, drug addicts, and gamblers. All of them are as poor as the poorest church mice. They have nowhere to go and nothing in their stomachs, so they're practically starving."

Alison no longer feels hungry. Even her flu seems to feel better, and she has stopped coughing. As she carries plates of hot dinner out to the crowd, she spies her three-year-old son playing with the other children, running between tables as they play hide-and-seek together.

'As long as the kids are safe and happy, then I'm happy, too,' Alison thinks to herself as she brings out a rich dessert of early Christmas pudding and cream. 'When everyone's finished eating, I'll help with the washing up. Then I'll have something hot and ask Maggie if she knows of a safe place we can stay for the night.'

Across the crowded room, Alison sees the older SVP sergeant also working by bussing dirty dishes back to the kitchen. Back and forth, the old volunteer marches, clearing one table after another until Alison can see the sweat dripping from her chin.

"Let me help," Alison says to her new friend, hurrying to Maggie and picking up a dirty plate from a table. "I'll bring the plates and bowls, and you bring the glasses and cups. We'll get this whole place cleaned up before you can sing a pre-Christmas Christmas carol."

"What's your favorite carol?" Maggie asks as she carries an armload of glasses on a tray into the kitchen. "Mine is 'Silent Night.'"

As Alison follows with a tray full of plates and cutlery, she thinks about Maggie's question. "I love all of them, especially 'Oh Come All Ye Faithful,'" she says. "They remind me of Pookey, my partner. We missed last Christmas together, and oh, how we all miss him being home." Maggie looks back to see that tears stream from Alison's eyes at the memory.

"Where is he?" Maggie asked. "Did you split up?"

"Oh no, not that," Alison whispers as she starts to sob, both hands moving to her face. "He was diagnosed with early onset, acute Alzheimer's. He's in Cork University Hospital, and I got to see him only one time before his memory of me vanished. Two days ago, I went to see him, and when he threw his breakfast at me in a pique of anger that I could not understand, the nurses gently told me I couldn't come back until he seemed better, which might not ever happen again."

Alison shakes again as the memory of that last visit comes flooding back. Then she looks up at Maggie, her face filling with dread. "If everyone thinks that I'm insane and word gets out and the staff at the hospital finds out, I might never see my sweetheart again!"

Then Alison bends over, sobbing until she is on her knees. "Oh, gersha," Maggie cries, tears also streaming from her eyes. "I'll say an entire rosary tonight for you, your Pookey, and your entire family. God will help you as the Bible says and as Our Lady promises every time we pray the Angelus or do a Novena to Saint Martha."

Alison looks up and stops crying, hope filling her eyes. "Pookey and I prayed the Angelus together every morning and night. And I do a Novena each and every Tuesday morning that God will cure him and bring him back to us. Oh, Maggie, I miss him so much!" And Alison breaks down again.

Later, after she has dinner, Alison feels better. She sits with the homeless and sings old Irish traditional music and 1916 Revolution songs with them. She even has a dance with Maggie to the tune of a fiddler as he plays an old Irish jig. When they are finished and as the crowd starts to leave, Maggie glances at Alison and knows from the worry in her eyes and on her face that she has nowhere to sleep tonight.

"You were fecked out, you and the children, by your landlord?" Maggie asks disdainfully. "What kind of man is that to throw you out on such a cold night. It's freezing outside. Temps are forecast to drop to well below zero. Is the landlord that heartless?"

Alison shakes her head and tries to smile. "His name is Tom. He couldn't help me though he's a dear friend. When Pookey got ill, Tom even took me to the hospital in his car anytime I asked. But you're right, Maggie. We've nowhere to stay. Is there a place that you know of, somewhere warm and safe, where I could place the kids? Fostering would be better than starving, at least until I sort myself out."

Maggie stands back, appalled. "But you're a wonderful mother! No, no," she tuts. "You can stay right here in the shop while *together* we sort out this mess. Right now, you need all the friends you can find. Now come with me," and Maggie leads Alison to a back room where donated furnishings are kept. "See, there's a wide double bed, enough for you and your kids. Over here," she continues, pointing, "is a pile of clean duvets, sheets, pillows, and more blankets. Come on, I'll help make up the bed. Then you can feed the twins and give that beautiful young son of yours a snack from the kitchen. Then I'll go home and you can get some sleep."

A few minutes later, while Alison breast-feeds her twins, Maggie serves them tea in fine donated China while Tim drinks milk from a brand-new glass and eats a few biscuits which the old Sergeant, now a close friend, also brought in. As the women sup at their tea, Maggie looks up with the fire of defiance in her eyes.

"Tomorrow is Friday, the last day of the week. The banks will be closed over the weekend," the old woman says, brushing her thick gray hair out of her dark green eyes. "I know a solicitor who will help us pro bono. Tomorrow, the three of us will march into the branch like the Three Musketeers. Well fight that idiot bank manager with knowledge and reason rather than hate, hunches, and lack of information. I give you my word, Alison, tomorrow by five, you'll be back in your warm flat."

When the old woman finishes, she lets herself out the front door, locking it. Alison changes into a warm nightgown Maggie gave her from a pile of brand-new donated clothing. Seeing that her kids are all asleep, she first tucks them in bed, then gets down on her knees.

"Oh my Mother, my Lady, my miracle worker, and the woman that I always turn to in time of need, please listen to the prayer I pray." Alison bows her head and prays her evening Angelus. When she finishes, she crawls into bed beside her kids.

"Pookey," she says, looking at the ceiling and swearing she can see her loving partner. "I know you're listening. Here's a kiss just for you." Alison kisses the back of her hand three times, then turns on her side, hugs all her children to her, and begins rubbing her elder son's ear, just as she did to Pookey to put him to sleep.

"See?" Alison whispers into the darkness. "I can feel your ear. Sleep well, my Pookey. I'll talk to you in the morning."

And with that, Alison goes to sleep knowing that the time for fear and sadness has passed. For tomorrow will be a great celebration because Maggie will help guard her back. Together, they will confront Brian the tyrant bank manager and resolve the entire mess. At that final thought, Alison rolls over once again and falls asleep with a smile of hope on her lips.

***

The next morning, the skies have cleared and sunlight streams through the windows. When she wakes, Alison is more determined to confront Brian than the night before. She glances at her phone. It is already nine o'clock, and she hurries to dress to be at the bank just before 10:00 a.m. When she sees the SVP ladies making breakfast for the homeless, she asks one of them if they can keep an eye on Tim and the twins for just a few minutes. She has to talk to the branch manager, but it won't take long at all. Then Maggie and Sally come in together. Alison whispers her plans to her best friend and promises that *everything* for *everybody* will work out this morning.

"What do you mean by everybody?" Sally asks. "Do you mean me?"

"Especially you," Alison says, and gives her friend a huge hug. "And that's a promise." Then she motions Maggie toward a far corner so they can talk.

"Maggie, thank you for coming to the bank with me this morning. I know that together we can successfully confront the bank manager. Just so you know, I also want you there to remember Brian's reaction to what we say to him. One day, I'll ask you to testify in court when I sue Brian and BAI Bank."

"You're going to sue them?" Maggie asks. "Isn't that going too far?"

"Are you kidding? They've humiliated me and deprived my children. As to suing them, I'm convinced I'll win. Depending on the size of the judgment, I'll share my winnings with every single person and organization I care about, including the Saint Vincent de Paul and your shop and the poor you serve so well."

At exactly 10:00 a.m., Alison and Maggie are the first through the door of the branch. As the pair stride in, the first thing they do is ask a BAI teller to help them for a moment. "Can you print out my most recent statements for my current account as well as my Visa card?" Alison asks the teller. When the teller does so, and with those pieces of paper in hand, she marches into Brian's tiny office side by side with her sergeant.

Alison waves the papers in Brian's face then slaps the statements onto his desk.

"You think I'm crazy?" Alison states firmly. "You tell me that I'm purchasing a house or something substantial. Yet here are my most recent statements. See? All of them are *legitimate* transactions, and the balances have always been *positive*. Even the deposits for my single parent's allowance are real and you *still* won't let me have them."

Alison places her fists on her hips, glaring at him. "Brian, I think the whole thing is a coverup. Either you're stealing from the bank, or *you're* the one who's crazy. Now what do you think of that?"

As Brian's face turns bright red at the double accusation, Maggie leans over the desk, her face old like thunder. "Do you realize that our young Alison had to take a gift of two-hundred and fifty euro from Saint Vincent de Paul to tide her over, you're so much of an idiot? She and her three kids had to spend the night in our shop because they were evicted from their flat because *you* wouldn't allow her to collect her social welfare payment, which was enough money to pay her rent."

"I've come to a number of decisions, Brian, that are going to personally affect you and the bank," Alison states. "First, I've asked my GP to file Form Five of the 2001 Mental Health Act of Ireland. This forces you to take a mental health evaluation. In the event that you are found insane, you will spend at least three months in a psychiatric unit, and probably much more.

"Second, I'm suing you personally for stealing my money, causing me and my children hardship, and causing us emotional and physical distress. When I talk to my solicitor, which this kind woman is arranging pro bono," she continues, glancing gratefully at Maggie, "and when we find the facts of what you and the bank did to us, we're going to sue you and BAI bank management for *millions*. Then you'll be homeless and just as humiliated as I am."

Then the two turn and march back into the lobby, now crowded with customers. Brian follows them, his face flushed by worry, as he reacts to their plan to ruin him.

"Don't you *dare* talk to me like that!" Brian shouts. "You have no proof that I did anything wrong. I was only following the rules and advice of the bank and their managers."

Alison turns slowly. "Shut up, Brian. You don't have a leg to stand on. The next time I see you will be in court. By the way, Maggie has agreed to act as a witness. With all the evidence I've got, it will be easy to win. So see you then, Brian. Toodles and have a really nice day!"

As the pair turn toward the door, two sirens wail in the distance, coming closer. Alison glances back at Brian, whose face has drained completely of color.

"I told you I called the cops, didn't I, Brian? That's them coming right now. They're coming along with five beefy goons who will place a straitjacket on you and take you immediately to the psychiatric ward for that evaluation. See you when you get out, Brian, when you are forced to appear in court. And just so you know," Alison says with a final riposte, "when I win, I'm going to take care of my kids, help all my friends and neighbors, and donate heavily to the SVP. And you know what? I'll do that with *your money* that I'll take from you when I win in court following our civil action, not the bank's cash. I've got better ideas for the bank's money. I'll set up a trust for the homeless and poor. But as to poor Brian? *Why you get absolutely nothing except grief and hardship for the rest of your life.*"

The End

ABOUT ALISON

Alison rarely talks about this true-life experience. One morning, however, woken by nightmares, she phoned me because I was a good friend and she trusted me. We sat over a glass of wine for over three hours as she recounted this tale of redemption and invincibility. Alison is a terribly bright, courageous, and determined professional woman now working for a large American East Coast university as a full professor.

Much of this story is fact. However, all names have been changed. There really is a squalid set of flats in Dublin's inner city in which Alison lived with her three now-grown children. There really is an apartment manager, (Tom is not his real name), who tried to help her out but was almost fired by the apartment owners, a giant corporation who bought the buildings for almost nothing, when they came to believe that Alison could not pay her back rent. There really is an SVP sergeant who gave Alison some cash and put her and her kids up for the night. And there really is a professor, previously employed at her university, who convinced a retired head of department (not in engineering) to fire her for being insane. Her Irish university convinced my friend to take a mental health examination. Having done so, Alison proved that she was not insane but rather one of the sanest people around (just as Tom says in the story). Alison successfully sued not only the bank manager but also the bank. She also sued for all three children, also winning in court. The judge, adjudicating on the ruling, stated it was one of the cruelest cases he had ever heard. Following the judgment, Alison really did give heavily to her neighbors and friends, her kind landlord, and the SVP.

Alison eventually completed her university degree at a prestigious university on the West Coast of the United States. She currently lives with her husband, Matthew, the father of her three children. (He really does have the nickname Pookey and was diagnosed with Early Onset Alzheimer's years ago. Due to effective medication and treatment, he is still alive and again realizes the depth of his love for Alison.) Having grown apart while Mat was in the hospital for several years with Alzheimer's disease, Alison chose to care for him at home. A few years ago, the happy couple announced the birth of another set of twins—this time boys.

WRITING A BESTSELLING NOVEL FOR ONLINE PUBLICATION

A How-to Guide White Paper
by Tom Richards: <u>www.tomrichards.ie</u>

BEFORE WE GET STARTED – A SPECIAL WARNING!

I spent all day yesterday rewriting what I thought would turn out to be Lesson Three. I spent hours on it, rewriting and polishing, making it right for all of thee. Each hour I saved it and before I went to bed, I saved it yet again. But I forgot to do something that I always do: TO BACK UP THE DOCUMENT BOTH ON AN EXTERNAL PRIVATE CLOUD AND A LOCAL DISC DRIVE.

When I woke up this morning and opened this document—DISASTER! LESSON THREE HAD VANISHED LIKE MAGIC! Now I'll have to spend all day doing it all over again!

The Big Lesson Here: The lesson for me and for all of us is pretty simple. At the end of every day, BACK UP YOUR WORK. The technology is cheap and easy to set up. Most word documents we write—even the longest manuscripts—should be backed up both locally and externally EVERY SINGLE DAY. There are a number of really cheap options to do this:

Local drives: include thumb drives and really inexpensive larger drives. You can buy them at Walmart or online for a few bucks.

External backups: are even cheaper. Use Google Drive (which also allows you to collaborate with someone else—such as your editor—on your work). Some new operating systems, like the latest version of Windows 10, provides for free OneDrive for Windows. This is supposed to automatically back up your work on a constant basis.

In my case, OneDrive didn't work yesterday, and I still don't know why. The other lesson is this: nothing is completely reliable. In my case, I wasted a full day. Don't be the same kind of idiot I was. I learned my lesson and will never do it again. Back it all up right now! For more information, Google "how to back up my Word documents." —Tom

What's Our <u>First</u> Mission? To Learn: How to write a chapter breakdown using my next novel for an adult audience, Misplaced Lovers, as an example.

But First, a Note to My Friends from Tom Richards:

Dear all,

Back fourteen or fifteen years ago, I had the opportunity to teach second-year students a course in screenwriting at Ireland's National University of Ireland, Maynooth. There, I discovered that they taught me more than I taught them.

Writing, as we all know, is an exercise in discipline and extraordinary frustration. We write and write and think we're never going to finish. But if you stick to it you will.

Due to the success of my first novel for adults, *Dolphin Song*—and I still can't believe it!—many of you have asked me, "What does it take to be a successful writer?" Sitting yer butt in a chair every day for more than a year is one thing, but actually *producing something that sells* is something else altogether.

In this white paper, "Writing a Bestselling Novel for Online Publication," I will take an approach rather different from the similar paper I wrote and published for *Dolphin Song*: "Cracking the Global Online Book Market: A How-To Guide." (That first paper is still available right here: https://drive.google.com/drive/folders/1rXWzOTBaj8r3PfhPWLFkIHqq6pz_XSMw?usp=sharing.)

In this case, I'll add to this paper as I complete each section of this new book-writing challenge: from *premise to character backstories, character arcs, and synopses*; to each *section* (there are four in this case); to each *sequence* (there are only still eight, just like a Hollywood screenplay), and we'll just see how it goes, because it will be loaded with mistakes.

P.S. If you catch any errors, please let this two-headed kangaroo know all about it!

So let's start from the very beginning, which is a very good place to start.

Here, we find the critical importance of the *premise*:

<u>LESSON NUMBER ONE—Let's Make a Start</u>

The First Step: Writing the Premise

First things first: I must explain that I started working on *Misplaced Lovers (ML)* over EIGHT YEARS AGO. I worked on it side by side with *Dolphin Song*, and I'm no Luke Skywalker, let me tell you. George Lucas worked on a couple of projects at once. He's BRILLIANT; I'm not.

But the point is this: I've worked my tail off, writing and editing, and writing and rewriting what is, after all, only a ROAD MAP to help me write the actual novel. It seemed never-ending, but now it seems finally done. When I'm all set, in a week or two, I'll begin the actual writing of the novel.

Another necessary explanation: in that the novel is magical realism, sort of a cross between a *Midsummer Night's Dream* by Shakespeare and something like *Cat in the Hat*, I've decided to write this in iambic pentameter to help me find the actual VOICE of the book. More on that below.

So without further ado,
Let's get started with
the premise as the
centerpiece of the shoe (ha-ha!) I mean *show*!

The *premise* is where we all start: for novels, it's usually a *one-paragraph* sort of explanation of the story which introduces the primary *protagonist*, the protagonist's challenge, which he or she must overcome, the *antagonist*, which does his or her best to ruin the protagonist's dreams, and a bit about the story, including the final *denouement* (no surprises here for your readers, which can include agents and publishers). It should also be written to allude to the *voice* of your novel—that is, the song, which are the notes or symphonic melody of the characters in which you will write the novel—and to be honest, that is very hard to do!

So I'll get down to it: after over one hundred tries, here's mine. Which means: it took me a great deal of time. I didn't give up. Don't you either!

Let me know what you think. —Tom

Finally, My Premise for *Misplaced Lovers!*

Grace Upendo (32) is a sexually-abused Black African. Full of fear and unwilling to reach out to those who could help heal her scarred heart, she finally meets the man of her dreams, **Sean Hope**. But when Sean understands how damaged she is, and despite his great love for her, he comes to realize that to heal her, he must leave her. When Grace finally gains the courage to escape from **Jester Jones**, an abusive Australian sailboat owner, she begins a frightening voyage of new discovery through stormy seas to an uncharted island only 150 nautical miles from Brisbane. There, in this land of lakes, streams, stunning wind-swept beaches, and tall trees, she begins to find new hope. On the island an adventure begins with a magical play, *Misplaced Lovers*. Its cast of characters, all animals and insects and talking bees, too, even includes a talking two-headed kangaroo. But when they begin to stage a raucous play based on Shakespeare's *Midsummer Night's Dream*, Grace soon discovers she cannot understand it. Filled with confusion, she is taken to Fish School by a pod of talking dolphins. There, beneath the churning waves, she finally learns her lesson: she can talk to the magical animals and even the two-headed roo! Having found the key, she is taken ashore, and finally asleep, she dreams of a door. Behind it is the roo, the talking kangaroo, who turns out to be Sean, her misplaced lover.

Misplaced Lovers is a cross-genre story of romantic fantasy and magical realism, in the same style as *The Life of Pi or The House of the Spirits*. This is the author's second novel for an adult audience.

Lesson Two: Chapter Breakdown

A chapter breakdown includes (at least for *Lost Lovers*):

1.   Cover—includes an illustration to emphasize the story.

2.   The *primary dramatic question* of the story that is compelling enough to encourage readers to read page after page? I think it's

Will Grace find enough courage to leave Brisbane and her captivity to journey to the uncharted island and find her misplaced lover, Sean Hope?

Part I—Title and Illustration Here (aka Act One)

Two more notes:

1. Always add an illustration at the beginning of each section to visually emphasize the tone of the story.

2. *Part one* goes from the very beginning of the book to the end of this part, also called the *point of departure*—or where Grace begins her *own* voyage of learning by escaping her captivity, which is the title of the part.

Grace's primary character arc: from scared and scarred by the past to finding the courage enough to steal the Australian's yacht and escape— that is, this is what she must learn to do and how she must act to achieve this part of her creative arc.

Now, let's finally get going with lesson two:

Sequence One (of eight in the total story)

Sequence title: Captivity (And now the actual chapters. Remember, each chapter right now requires only a paragraph or two or three. No more than five!)

Chapter One

Location: at the pier; Brisbane, Australia; morning (The pier is crowded with summer tourists/)

Grace is working on the yacht *Lost Love*, getting it ready for the tourists who will soon climb aboard. Dressed in an unbecoming nautical costume she is forced to wear by her employer, Grace pulls out a fold-down table and graces it with a snow-white tablecloth. Next, she lays out a meal just for two: there's the best of china and real silverware. Then a main dish of prawns with green noodles topped with a lovely thick sauce. Next a dessert of pudding cups capped with strawberries and whipped cream. Finally, she places on the table a bucket holding a bottle of chilled champagne and beside it two crystal glasses. Finished, she thinks, she spins from the table, inadvertently brushing the glasses with her elbow. They topple from the table and shatter on deck. And as they do Jester Jones, the yacht's Australian owner, dressed all in white, runs out from the cabin (where he'd been napping to let Grace do all the work).

"Don't you know those were *real* crystal and expensive, you fool!" he shouts at poor Grace. "I got them from a friend in Delhi—I suspect you don't even know where that is. Now snap to it and clean up that mess before the arrival of our guests!"

As he slinks off the deck, two tourists clamber aboard, but only one couple, both dressed in misfit outfits the characters might wear on television's *Gilligan's Island* (the TV Series), which are a sight to behold!

The male tourist (Huxley Bullak) is dressed like a fancy, privileged sailboat captain complete with navy coat and silly captains cap, while his idiot wife (Carliss Bullak) wears nothing but the best that Oxford Street can provide. (She thinks she's stunning even though she's anything but.) They've heard the ruction and see Grace's humiliation, but despite that, Bullak orders Grace:

"You, Princess!" he mewls, thinking it's a joke, but it's anything but. "Take my coat and my hat. Now pronto," he claps.

As Grace strides to comply, Jester orders Grace to cast off the boat. Caught between the two orders, Grace doesn't know what to do. With the guest's coat and hat hanging helplessly, one in each hand, Jester marches by her, casting off himself.

As the tourists watch with amusement, the boat moves away from the pier, but Grace's humiliation is anything but dear.

END OF CHAPTER.

Notice how short the chapter breakdown is? Remember, it's only a roadmap. I'll write nothing like it or just maybe I will! Who knows at this point? This is only the start of the voyage.

AND REMEMBER: EVERYTHING CAN CHANGE, SO DON'T BE TOO HARSH ON YOURSELF. IT'S THE WRITING THAT'S IMPORTANT, NOT ANYTHING ELSE. Just do it—and you'll be A-OK. On that, I can promise but only on that

Chapter Two

Location: At sea, later that morning

The waters are choppy, the strong winds uncertain. Grace, still at sea due to her earlier argument with Jack, is ordered by him to trim the sail when the winds turn around. She tries to comply, but a wave hits the boat. As the sailboat rocks, Carliss squeals as Huxley gets sick over the side.

Jack screams at Grace as she fumbles with the ropes: "You should know how to do this! You've had enough lessons from me. You should know this yacht from stem to stern and back again."

"You gave me one lesson!" Grace retorts. "How dare you give out to me!" and she turns again to the wayward sail. As the boat rocks again, Jack runs to the wheel inside the boat (INT cabin). When a stronger wave hits, it knocks him, and he loses control of the tiller. As the wheel spins, the tourists topple, Dom Pérignon and whipped cream all over them!

At the commotion, Grace composes herself and then flies to the wheelhouse to take appropriate action. She grasps the big wheel and turns the *Loved Lost* west-southwest into the teeth of the storm and the boat, why she's bucking again!

Grace takes action again.

A third wave hits, much bigger than the rest. It wrests the wheel from Grace's control.

This brings you up to *the incipient incident:* When Grace is *forced* to make a decision about staying on the yacht, the *Lost Lover*, or going east or west. (BTW, if she goes west, the yacht sinks—and that's the end of the story.)

Now, dear writer, you've only seven sequences to go. (Remember, there are eight sequences in a screenplay, novel, or even a stage play, at least in a traditionally constructed Hollywood story—which, by the way, is more likely to be published!)

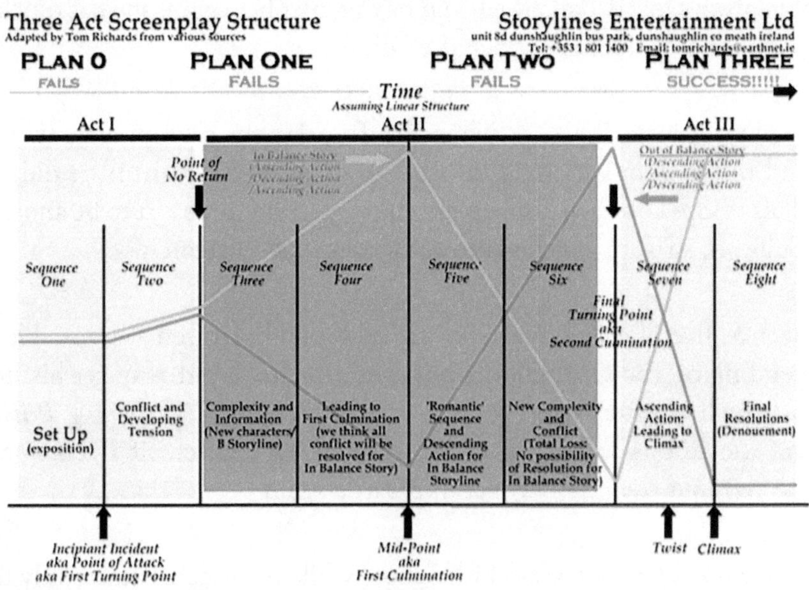

LESSON THREE: Remaining Story Structure

From here on in it really is quite easy (sometimes, anyway). Surge right to the *point of departure*; otherwise, your audience will get bored. In *Lost Lovers*, the point of departure is when Grace boldly steals the yacht and sails to the Magical Island.

In films, it's even easier to find. Take the film *Peter Pan* with Robin Williams. When the children fly to Peter's mystical land—that's the point of departure.

Now it's two sequences until the *midpoint,* maybe three to six chapters if you're writing a book. The midpoint sort of fools readers and viewers. The star of the piece, says Robin Williams, seems to get what they're looking for. Maybe, in this case, Tinkerbell is caught by Captain Hook. Robin always loved Tinkerbell, and having met her again, she has quickly departed. So he doesn't get her after all.

In *Saving Private Ryan,* it's when the Tom Hanks character *thinks* he's found the man he's looking for: the surviving O'Sullivan. If he did, he and his troops could go home again. But that man turns out to be another O'Sullivan, so Tom and his men must continue the search.

Sequence five is called the *romantic sequence,* but often it's not. Here, depending on the screenplay, a boy who has met a girl may get his first kiss (which is often saved for the end of the story). In *Saving Private Ryan,* the troops sort of rest (the scene in the church, if I remember correctly), but then quickly get into battle again.

In *Lost Lovers,* Grace goes to Fish School while the Mechanicals study the play within a play, where they combine Shakespeare with something else. So often this sequence is preparation for what comes next, but it can't be too slow, or your audience may close the book and never pick it up again.

Let's now look at *sequence six.* For me, this is hard to write in that I'm often out of material until I get to *sequence seven,* which is the final battle.

Sequence six begins to gather the sometimes tangled stories and begins to draw them together as the story once again gains momentum. For instance, in *Lost Lovers,* Grace will again become attracted to a spider that is also her lover (Eee-gads! A spider? That's right, I say. For more info go to www.tomrichards.ie.) But anyway, gather the various stories together and start to tie them up.

In *Saving Private Ryan,* it's easy: they follow pretty much a single plot line, which is the premise of the entire story: Will Tom and his men find

O'Sullivan or not and rescue him from the hands of the Nazi army? In *Lost Lovers*, it's more difficult. The various plots are: Will Grace find her lover, and if so, will they fall in love again? And will the Mechanicals pull off a stage play provisionally entitled *Lost Love?* And what ever happened to the captain (who is a real prick) of the *Lost Lover*, the yacht? Will the yacht be refloated because it sank when Grace came to the Magical Island? What happened to the English tourists who are still in Australia, or will we ever see them again?

So you can write a story focusing on only a single story (called a single-strand story) or with multiple plots: plot A, subplot B, C, and D—etc. It just depends how complicated you want to make your story.

Sequence seven is easy to explain. This leads to the *main story climax.* In *Saving Private Ryan*, it's where Tom and his troops find O'Sullivan, having just fought a battle, and now they have to continue to do so.

This is where a *complication* comes in. Tom has found O'Sullivan. He must take him back to safety. However, there's this battle, and O'Sullivan point-blank refuses to go. So we have to wait to see if O'Sullivan survives or not. If he does not, then Tom's work has been done in vain: he's lost a whole mess of friends and soldiers. If O'Sullivan dies, all that work and bloodshed will be in vain.

Then TOM dies, not O'Sullivan. And the battle at the bridge is over, so Tom knows—as he passes away—that his mission is a success.

In *Lost Lovers*, it's where (I'm not going to tell you: That's a spoiler! Buy the book at www.tomrichards.ie and find out for yourself.)

In *Sleepless in Seattle,* it's where the lovers finally meet on top of the Empire State Building. (BTW: Sleepless is unusual because it does *not* have a *sequence eight*, at least not really. It's where these two lovers and Tom's son become united as a single family.)

So you see how easy it is? Everything, all along the voyage of the screenplay, points to, and comes down to, the *climax*, the end of *sequence seven*.

But what about *sequence eight?* In films, it's usually very short, only a few minutes. Often it's where the boy kisses the girl, or where friends meet after some sort of battle and extremely difficult final complication to say either hello or goodbye forever.

Whatever it is, it's small. In my novel *Dolphin Song*, the three protagonists, Dawn, Michael, and Jason, travel west into a setting sun, having all been turned into dolphins, and we know that they are finally content following one hell of a battle to get this far. We as the reader also know that this story could well continue.

So whatever you do with *sequence eight*, make it small. If it's a film, it's only two or three minutes (one page of written screenplay is equal to one minute of screen time). If a novel, maybe a small final chapter.

And Finally:

Whoever you are and wherever you are, if you're writing a story, I know it's difficult, but I'm with you. Keep chugging away, maybe even one page a day. Put your arse in that chair for a few hours every day. Being a successful writer starts with hard work, diligence, discipline, and taking time to think things through.

But keep on writing, even if you get stuck, and God willing, you'll have a bestseller on your hands just as I have with *Dolphin Song*.

I wish thee well. Blessings. Tom

For more information and private tutoring in story creation, contact me:

<u>Tomrichards141@gmail.com</u>
Tel: +353866004475
I leave a bio below so you know my qualifications to teach the craft of storytelling:

Film
Gotcha—a puppetry TV series for RTE One Ireland
Missing—a one-hour TV series for Italian TV
Merlin: the Magic Begins—two-hour feature film

Novels and Non-Fiction
Always Come Home
Dolphin Song
Happiness & Heartbreak
Lost Lovers
The Lost Scrolls of Newgrange
Hotfoot
Hotfoot Two: Lucky's Revenge
The Den Show tie-in for television (illustrated book for children)
Sue the Two Headed Rue and You (Personalized storybook—in progress)
Survivors Guide to Living in Ireland (non-fiction)
Various horror short stories for Poolbeg Press, Ireland

My training includes a variety of storytelling programs, including Step by Step, eQuinoxe Germany, Arista, and many others.

An Afterthought

Creating something as wonderful as an anthology penned by great writers (and I leave that last phrase out regarding myself) was an honor. A special thanks goes, of course, to all of the people who submitted manuscripts and were chosen for publication by our Storylines Entertainment editorial board. Special acknowledgment must go to Bill Leece, English educator extraordinaire.

To Carmel Murray, Frank McQuaid, Aoife Murphy, and the entire team at the Bantry Psychiatric Unit, I once again give you thanks for your care, love, and concern.

Enter Our 2023 Short Story, Play and Poetry Anthology Competition

This first volume announces the annual Storylines Entertainment Ltd. Anthology Competition for Known and Unknown Writers across the globe.

To enter our 2023 competition, send your short story, play, or selection of poetry to tomrichards141@gmail.com.

We promise to notify you of our jury results for publication. Each writer chosen for publication will receive a small reward. This year's prize was US$100 per selected author.

With so many thanks to all of you for entering this year's Anthology Competition.

Tom Richards
November 2022
Eyeries, Beara Peninsula, Ireland P75 A342